# Fatal Intentions
Fatal Cross Live, Book 4
By Theresa Hissong

Copyright © 2020 Theresa Hissong

## Disclaimer:

This book is a work of fiction. Any resemblance to any person, living or dead is purely coincidental. The names of people, places, things, songs, bands are all created from the author's mind and are only used for entertainment. Any mention of a song, or band, in the book, has been given proper credit for use.

This book is for adults 18 and older only; due to content.

**Cover Design:**
Custom eBook Covers

**Editing by:**
Heidi Ryan
Amour the Line Editing

**Cover Model:**
Eric Ten Brink

**Cover Photographer:**
Eric Battershell

***Contents:***
Prologue
Chapter 1
Chapter 2
Chapter 3
Chapter 4
Chapter 5
Chapter 6
Chapter 7
Chapter 8
Chapter 9
Chapter 10
Chapter 11
Chapter 12
Chapter 13
Chapter 14
Chapter 15
Chapter 16
Chapter 17
Chapter 18
Chapter 19
Chapter 20
Chapter 21
Chapter 22
Chapter 23
Chapter 24
Epilogue

*Dedication:*
To:
Baby Cash Ryan Vickery
April 8, 2016 – April 9, 2016
This one's for you, little man.
Keep rocking out in heaven, teaching those angels how it's done.

To:
Courtney & Randall Vickery
There is nothing more unyielding than a parent's love. Your strength will guide you in the years to come. Your faith will help you heal. Your love will help you remember.

With all of my love,
Theresa

*Prologue*
*Cash*
*Remembering*

*The show had been a success, and we'd partied like it was our last night on this earth. With a tray of cocaine and several bottles of pills sitting on the coffee table of our suite, I took the band whore to my room for a little fun.*

*She was a high-class hooker, but in my drug-fogged brain, I didn't care. She stroked my long hair just the way I liked it, sucked my cock like she'd been trained by a professional, and I thought her brown eyes held a mystery only I could uncover.*

*The morning came with fear as my singer and best friend overdosed right in front of my eyes. Ace was vomiting blood, and I was forced to call for help. Even through my high, I knew we'd hit rock bottom.*

*The weeks in rehab were the worst. My body had gone through pain like I'd never felt. The detox was real, and I'd made a promise to myself that if I made it, I would never touch drugs or alcohol again.*

*The day we were released, everyone started their new lives, and we made a plan for our future. It took a month for us to get set up with our sponsors and find a new balance. During that time, I loaded up my belongings and moved west of Seattle to a faraway place in the Olympic Peninsula.*

*I couldn't stay at my old house, because it brought back too many memories, and with that, the people I had let take advantage of me. Within a week, my drug dealer had shown up, offering me whatever he had. It took a lot of strength, but I sent him on his way.*

*Once we were settled into a sober life, we met one weekend at my new lake house and got down to work writing new material. The weekend turned into a week, and that week turned into a month. By the time we were ready to head into the studio, we'd found a new drummer and had written one of our best albums.*

# Chapter 1
## Cash

Boarding the plane to Los Angeles, I kept my sunglasses on and my long hair tucked securely in a knit cap to keep from being noticed. The tint on my glasses was so dark, I could watch my surroundings without anyone noticing if I made eye contact with them.

The stewardess smiled warmly as I took my seat. "Mr. Roberts, would you like a glass of champagne?"

"No, thank you," I replied, swallowing a lump in my throat. "I don't drink."

"I'm sorry," she replied with a bit of shock. "Water?"

"No, thank you," I answered with a half-smile. I wasn't worried about her knowing my name, because I was flying first class, and anyone who sat around me probably didn't care who I was, anyway. The disguise was just to get through the airport without being mobbed.

While we waited to depart, I pulled up the text my band mate, Braxton, had sent me half an hour ago.

*Check on Penny while you're in L.A. She's been acting weird lately.*

Penelope Keller was my drummer's twin sister. She'd been in Los Angeles for the filming of a new movie for the past few months. Braxton didn't tell me what was going on, but I had my suspicions. We all had our fair share of demons, and Penny was not without her own. Braxton's worry over his sister was warranted.

I had my own business there, and we'd taken a three-day break from finishing up our new album so I could finally go tie up some loose ends with my father's estate. It was the last place I wanted to be, but knowing I could see Penny made things a little brighter.

It'd been three years since I had found out about his passing from a breaking news story. Ace had called me and told me to look online.

*Howard Roberts, legendary guitarist, dead at age 57.*

He'd left everything to me, and I was resentful as hell. We'd never had a relationship. He'd chosen to walk out on my mom when I was a teenager, leaving her to fend for herself when he found fame and she was diagnosed with breast cancer.

I'd worked two jobs through high school, helping her pay the bills so we could keep the lights on in the one-bedroom apartment we shared. It bothered me that she slept on the couch while I had the lone bedroom to myself. I still had nightmares about it.

When she passed right after my twentieth birthday, he didn't even have the common decency to send flowers or even call to ask how I was doing. I hated him, and he knew it.

Shaking my head to dislodge the thoughts from my mind, I quickly sent an email to the estate lawyer, confirming our appointment for the next morning. My father's estate had been put into a trust after I had hired a company to sell off everything he'd ever owned.

The famous guitars were bought by a collector, and I hoped he made good use of them. The awards were also gone. I didn't want them. I didn't need a reminder of how he'd become such a celebrated guitarist and the general public had no clue what a piece of shit he really was.

As they closed the doors to the plane, I shot off a text to Penny.

*Hey, you. I'm flying out of Seattle right now, and I'll be in L.A. tonight. We should have dinner.*

I powered down my phone and closed my eyes as we taxied out to the runway. The flight from Seattle to LAX wasn't going to take long, and I'd confirm plans with her when I was on the ground in California.

Taking Penny to dinner wasn't going to be a

hardship. I'd known her ever since her brother had joined my band after we'd all finished rehab. I'd be a liar if I said I hadn't noticed her. She wasn't hard to miss.

We'd flirted several times, but Braxton had always been there to remind me to keep my hands off his sister, because he knew how I was when it came to attractive women. He must have really been worried about Penny if he chose me to be the one to check up on her.

When we landed, I powered up my phone and frowned when there was no reply from Penny. After getting my bags, I rented a car to take to the hotel close to the lawyer's office. I didn't plan on being in L.A. for long. I just wanted to get it over with and go home.

Dropping my bag on the couch in my room, I sat heavily on the bed as I thumbed through all of the paperwork the lawyer had sent me. I rubbed my temples as I scanned the information again. I knew he was famous, but I didn't realize how smart he really was until I saw the amount of money I was inheriting.

Being his only child, I was going to be set for life, but I wasn't going to let that change me. My band was doing amazingly well, and I had my own small fortune to live on, but the amount was so much more than I ever expected.

With the excesses my father loved to indulged in, you would've thought he'd used up a lot of his money, but he hadn't. He was smart and invested early. Seeing the records pissed me off even more for my mother who had struggled after he left. She'd been too sick to take him to court for child support. So, the responsibility had fallen on me.

My phone pinged beside me, and I took a deep breath to calm my nerves. My parents were gone, and despite my hatred of my father, I had to look forward.

*I am on set until seven. If you'd like to come by, I can leave you a pass at the gate.*

After my response, I took a quick shower and got ready for the evening. By the time I called down to valet to have my rental brought around, it was nearing six o'clock. Los Angeles traffic was a nightmare, but I made it to the studio with ten minutes to spare.

"I'm here to see Penelope Keller," I told the guard at the gate. With a weathered smile, he took my driver's license and searched for my name on his clipboard.

"Ah, here you are, Mr. Roberts," the old man replied with a smile, handing me two items. "Keep this pass in your car and the other one is a sticker for your shirt. Wear it at all times. Ms. Keller is at studio

74."

I removed the backing on the sticker and stuck it to my black cotton shirt instead of my leather jacket. Rubbing my hands on my pants, I pulled the door open and walked inside where I was met by a security guard.

"Mr. Roberts?" the guard asked.

"I'm here to see Ms. Keller," I replied.

"Follow me." The guard left his post and turned right down a hallway with several doors marked for actors and actresses. At the end of the hallway, he knocked on a door labeled with her name. A woman answered and stepped aside to allow me entrance.

"Penelope is finishing her scene and should be here any minute," the tall, dark-haired woman advised, holding out her hand. "I'm her assistant, Terri."

"Hello, Terri," I greeted, releasing her hand as soon as possible.

"Have a seat," she offered as her eyes drank me in. "Can I get you anything?"

"No, thank you," I replied and sat on the green velvet sofa by the wall. To my left was a makeup station, and on the other side of the room, a rack of clothing sat by a door leading into what I assumed was a bathroom.

Terri fluttered around, cleaning up the makeup

station and bagging up the trash for the day. She left without a word, but returned a few minutes later with a folder, placing it on the makeup counter.

When the door opened again, I looked up to see Penny entering with her eyes cast downward. Her long, brown hair was perfectly styled in waves around her petite face, but I couldn't see her clearly because of the shadow it cast on her face. Narrowing my eyes, I stood quickly, catching her off guard. She righted her features and a huge grin spread across her face.

"Cash, you're here."

"I'm here," I replied and walked over to give her a hug. Her assistant looked at me in question as we embraced, but I was concerned by the look on her face. I tucked my face into her hair to whisper so Terri couldn't hear. "Who put that sadness in your eyes, babe?"

"Um," she mumbled as she pulled back from our hug. She glanced over at Terri and gave her head a slight shake. "So, dinner?"

"Whenever you are ready," I replied, feeling a bit protective of her. She obviously didn't want to talk about whatever was bothering her in Terri's company, and I immediately wanted to tell the woman to get the fuck out of Penny's dressing room, but I didn't. It wasn't my place to fire her. Penny didn't know how deep my need to protect a woman went, and I really wasn't in a place to fire the woman, but I wanted to. Hell, I'd hire Penny someone she could trust. God knew I had enough of my father's fucking money to do it.

"Let me get out of these clothes," she announced, a soft blush painting the tops of her cheeks as she picked up the hem of the dress she was wearing and dropped it back to the floor like it was a heavy burden she was ready to shed. I nodded for her to continue and retook my spot on the couch.

Terri assisted Penny in changing out of her outfit before excusing herself for the night. The assistant gave me one last glance before closing the door. I stared at the back of the door while Penny gathered her things, wondering why she didn't trust the woman.

"You're going to have to choose a place, because I am of no help," I shrugged, and held the door open as she grabbed the manilla folder off the desk. She dropped it in her sleek, black bag and hoisted the strap over her shoulder. "Here, let me."

She handed over the bag, and then we were off. The other actresses we met on our way out said their goodbyes and well wishes for the weekend. Penny smiled when they approached, but it immediately died on her lips the moment they were out of sight. I didn't need to be told she was having problems on the set, because I could read it all over her face.

The security guard held the door for us as we walked out, and Penny gave him thanks with a real smile…a smile I recognized. If the fucking security guard was her only friend there, I knew she was miserable.

The headlights on my rented BMW flashed twice as I approached the passenger side door. Penny kept quiet and slid into the seat. I hurried around to the driver's door and got in, cranking the car before looking over at her. She'd leaned her head back on the headrest and closed her eyes.

"Where to?" I asked.

"Anywhere, Cash," she said with exasperation. "Please, just get me out of here."

I didn't want to stick around the lot any longer than necessary. I pulled up the map to return to my hotel and sped out of the lot. The further away from the studio I got, the more she sat upright in her seat.

"So, are you going to tell me what the fuck I just witnessed back there?"

## Chapter 2
## Penny

Today had been hell. The tension on the set just continued to get worse, and my fucking co-star was a piece of shit. If I had to hear one more fucking time that he was going to look terrible next to a fat chick again, I was going to lose my shit.

"Long story short," I began, knowing Cash was only here by the request of my brother. He couldn't come save his twin sister, but he knew his bassist was going to be in town, so he enlisted Cash to come get the details. And the *only* reason I was telling him was because we had two more days of filming, and I would be done with Malcom Sterling, aka Sexiest Douchebag in Hollywood three years running. "Malcom hates me, and everyone working on this set thinks he can do no wrong."

"Why does he hate you?" Cash asked. I saw the grip he had on the steering wheel tightening.

I really wanted to forget it, but if I didn't send Cash home with news, then Braxton would be here before I could finish filming just so he could kick Malcom's ass into next year. Oh, who was I kidding? As soon as the reasoning left my lips, the whole damn band would be there first thing tomorrow.

"Ah, he doesn't think we are attractive together,"

I sighed, losing my bravery when he came right out and asked me. "Let's just forget it. I know my brother sent you to check on me. Just tell him I'll be done filming by mid-week. After that, I'll be home."

Cash quieted for a moment, and I watched him out of the corner of my eye. He was maneuvering around cars as he finally made his way onto the interstate. Immediately, we were stuck in traffic, and I closed my eyes again, only to have them open when he cursed under his breath. "Tell me what that motherfucker said, Penny."

"Cash, damn it." I paused, but I could feel his eyes upon me. I'd always been aware when the man was close. He gave off a warmth that my internal instincts wanted to latch onto like I was a damn animal. "Fine! He has an issue with my weight."

"Excuse me!" Cash bellowed, tightening the death grip he had on the wheel. He'd always been respectful toward me, knowing the hell I'd been through in my early twenties. "How could he think that? Penny, you are not overweight."

"I am compared to what I was several years ago, Cash," I admitted, looking at my lap. "Seriously, you don't have to get upset."

My demons were as addictive as the ones my brother and his band mates had been through all those years ago. Where Braxton was addicted to heroin, I preferred to stick my finger down my throat to throw up everything I consumed. I became addicted to the act to keep my figure down. It took some time after my brother and mom put me into a facility to help me overcome my addiction to learn how to eat and exercise right. My problem was the fact that my ancestors were probably robust women and their thickness trickled down to me through my genetics.

"I can't believe he said that to you." Cash had calmed, thankfully.

"Look, Cash," I sighed as I turned in my seat, "I'm the healthiest I've ever been, and I'm not as fat as Malcom says I am. He is just used to getting his way, and I'm not his typical co-star. Everyone else he's been in movies with are size zero. The only reason I haven't told everyone there to fuck off is because my producer has my back. She's amazing, because she reminds him every day that the movie was an adaptation of a book where the heroine was a size ten and it's told from the female character's point of view."

"So, you do have someone there who is good to you? Not just the old security guard at the door?" He seemed relieved when I gave him a smile and a nod.

"She's good to me," I promised. "This movie has changed my life already, and it's expected to be huge."

"I'm happy for you, Penny," he vowed and reached for my hand, giving it a tiny squeeze before letting go. "You deserve it."

"Speaking of life changing," I began, giving him a huge smile. "This new album is going to make waves, Cash."

"So, you've heard it?" he asked, but the smirk that played at the corner of his lips told me he already knew my brother had sent it.

"Of course, I have," I giggled. "The song, 'Despicable', is probably going to be my favorite song."

I wondered if he was going to ask me about their song, "Purge", and I was a little thankful when he didn't bring it up. They'd written a song about my time with bulimia. I'd heard it, and they had done an amazing job on it. It brought back a ton of memoires. The song itself was emotional, and even if you didn't know anyone who suffered from it, the music was sure to make you cry.

The song told a story of a young woman who suffered from the eating disorder, she drank too much, and basically had given up on life. She fought through her demons and came out the other side stronger and healthier in the end.

It was me…I was the reason for the song. Braxton had come to me one night with the pitch, wanting my blessing to go forward with the song. I'd read the lyrics before I listened to the demo, and by the end of it all, I was a blubbering mess in my brother's arms.

"We have a lot going on over the next few months," he said. "Tour is already being set up for the week of release, and we are going to have so many radio interviews that my head is spinning."

"You guys will do fine," I said, pointing to the next exit. "Get off here. I know a great Thai place."

He flipped on the blinker and got off where I'd indicated, turning right at the light. When we were a few blocks away, I reached into my bag and grabbed my flimsy hat and sunglasses while Cash retrieved his beanie from the dashboard. We both froze once we realized we were both covering ourselves.

"It's part of the job, huh?" I teased, but we both knew our lives had been inevitably changed the moment we took on our careers. I never thought I would need to hide from the paparazzi, but here I was, donning a disguise so I could have a nice, quiet meal with a friend.

*A hot as fuck friend.*

My mind drifted to a few summers ago at Ace's house while we were having a family cookout. Cash and I had done a lot of heavy flirting while my brother's back was turned. We'd slipped up once, and

Braxton had inserted himself physically between us for the next hour. After that, we hadn't really spent a lot of time together. I'd come to a show every now and then when they were in the area, but they were always busy.

"I have business here, and I don't want it to leak just yet," he cursed.

"Leak?" My hand automatically reached out to rest on his wrist. I knew what I'd done but I didn't pull away. "What's going on, Cash?"

"You knew who my dad was, right?" he asked, raising his brow.

"Yeah, of course," I laughed. "Who doesn't?"

"Well, I've been putting off getting my inheritance from his estate," he explained. "I'm meeting with the lawyer tomorrow."

"Oh, wow," I replied. Holy shit, his father was the most famous guitarist in recorded history. He was a legend.

"Yeah," he sighed. "Looks like I get daddy's money."

"That's just…" I paused. What was I going to say to that? But Cash looked almost pained about the meeting. "Why do you look so torn?"

"I hated him," he admitted. "He never won an award for being the best father, and I hadn't spoken to him since I was in a coke rage about seven years ago.

Even though I told him where to stick his fatherhood, he still left me everything, and I don't know why."

"I'm sorry, Cash." I frowned as I touched his hand. To hate your own father was saying a lot. Howard Roberts was known for his fast lifestyle, and from what I'd seen of Fatal Cross before they all went into rehab, Cash had been following in his footsteps.

"What did he say to you the last time you saw him?" I was honestly curious, and I hoped Cash didn't think I was prying.

"We actually played a festival with him," he admitted with a sarcastic laugh. "We were openers and basically a nobody in the music business, and he was there to headline the weekend. He was drunk, as usual, and I was coked out. He came at me about my mother. He said some things that pissed me off. If it wasn't for Ace, I would've been in jail that night."

"I'm sorry," I replied. I could tell Cash had a lot of resentment for his father, and to be honest, I didn't blame him.

I came from a very loving home, and after my father died, Braxton, my mom, and I grew stronger. Cash didn't have that. Braxton told me Cash had come from a severely broken home and his mother had died from some sort of cancer when he was in his early twenties, but that was the extent of my knowledge.

"It's okay, Penelope," he promised as we arrived at the restaurant valet in front of the building. He very rarely called me by my given name, and the sound of it falling from his lips sent a warmth to the center of my chest. "Let's eat, and then I'll take you home so you can get some rest."

"Let's do this." The valet opened my door first, offering his hand to assist me as I exited the vehicle. Thankfully, I'd worn a dark green pantsuit to work today, knowing Cash was going to be in town and would most likely want to get together for dinner. If it was any other day, I'd have worn something more casual since I had a driver to take me to and from the studio. No one would've seen me in my hoodie and leggings.

Cash handed the young man his keys and a tip, turning toward me to escort me inside. He placed his hand on my lower back and the warmth from his touch almost burned my skin. I couldn't remember a time when he had touched me that possessively and it made butterflies dance in my stomach. Hell, I could've been nervous because of our location, and knowing how bad the tabloids could be, if we were seen together, the headlines would explode.

Thankfully, the front of the place was void of cameramen. The sun had set right before we left the studio, and the temperatures were mild. I liked my home in Seattle where we had actual seasons. Los Angeles was fun for a trip, but what I really wanted to do was sit at my mom's kitchen table and watch the rain as it ran in rivulets down the windows while drinking a hot cup of coffee over a nonsense conversation with her.

    I'd even be happier with my grumpy brother in attendance.

## Chapter 3
## Cash

My hand tingled with awareness as I guided Penny toward the door. Thank fuck there were no cameras outside the building. I was pushing it being out in public in Los Angeles, let alone with Penelope Keller. The tabloids were vicious, and she'd already had her fair share of bullshit splashed across their pages. We didn't need to add my demons into the mix.

"Good evening," a hostess greeted. "Just the two of you?"

"Yes," I responded.

"Right this way."

The woman acted like she could care less as to who we were and turned to show us to our seats. For a Monday night, the place was almost to capacity, but that was normal for California.

"Your server will be right with you," she stated as if she'd said it a million times over.

I pulled out the chair for Penny and took my own after she was seated. By the time I sat down, a man in a deep purple suit approached with a bottle of wine. "Could I get you a glass of Merlot?"

"No, thank you," I replied and waited for Penny to answer.

"I'll just have water, no ice, please," she replied with a sweet smile.

"If you'd like a glass of wine, I don't mind," I said once the man had nodded and walked away. I didn't want her feeling uncomfortable about drinking around me.

"No, Cash. I really don't feel like having a drink tonight. Plus, red wine triggers my migraines." She shrugged and opened her menu. "I need to drink more water, anyway."

"Okay," I frowned. I didn't know she suffered from migraines.

We studied the menu for several minutes while we waited on our drinks. I couldn't keep my eyes focused on the selections, because I kept catching myself watching her as she read over the menu. Her long, brunette hair held just enough of a curl that I felt my fingers itch to let one lock of it twirl around my fingers.

*Jesus. Fuck!*

I could *not* get involved with my drummer's sister. It would cause issues in our band if things went south. Braxton had warned me away from her so many times, I lost count. He had every right to be concerned. I was a recovering alcoholic and drug abuser. My list of escapades still came back to haunt me in every town we played a show.

I had changed after I walked out of that treatment facility, though. With a new lease on life, I ditched everyone and everything that had to do with my former self. I changed my phone number and moved out to Port Angeles, almost three hours from Seattle. I liked my peace and quiet out there, and it kept me out of trouble.

I'd recently bought a three-bedroom condo in Seattle, close to the studio, for the times we would be recording. It came furnished, and I planned on keeping it to use when I needed to be closer to the city.

"What would you like to order, sir?" the waiter asked, pulling me from my thoughts.

"Beef Pad Thai, medium heat, please," I announced.

"Ma'am?"

"Seared Ahi Tuna Salad, please," Penny ordered, folding the menu and handing it over. I didn't comment on her choice of food, and let it go. Braxton was always worried about her decision to go on a pescatarian diet. He didn't think she was getting the right amount of nutrients, but she had assured everyone it was healthy. She knew her body now that she'd been through the program. I wouldn't fault her for watching what she ate.

With her spotlight in Hollywood, it came with

body issues. The vultures of the tabloids were already on her about the estimated success of the movie she was starring in, and that alone kept her in the public eye. They were starting to follow her everywhere, and I'd been seeing the headlines. They shamed her for being a few pounds overweight, and they were causing her to be put in a hard position. Penny couldn't let it get to her, because she was doing everything the nutritionist was telling her to do.

"I can see the look in your eyes, Cash," she sighed heavily. "Pescatarian diets are healthy, and I chose it because of my migraine issues. I don't want to eat anything that will trigger an episode. I've found that I feel better eating this way."

"Braxton worries about you," I finally admitted.

"Oh, I know," she laughed. "I know he conned you into calling me and coming by to check on me."

"That's not entirely true," I admitted, relaxing a bit. "I wanted to see you."

A soft blush painted the tops of her cheeks, "I'm glad you did."

"Me, too, Penelope," I nodded. "Me, too."

After our dinner was served, I noticed it was nearing nine. "What time do you have to be at the studio tomorrow?"

"Seven," she scowled. "We have a few scenes to finish. I'm hoping we can get them done as soon as possible. I'd like to go home."

"I'm leaving on Wednesday," I said, folding my cloth napkin and setting it on top of the table as the waiter brought us our check. "If you are done and can get on my flight, I'll give you the information. I can drive you to your mom's house when we land."

"That would be much easier than hiring a car to take me home." She paused to think for a moment. "I'll let you know. I'm sure I will need to come back here in a few weeks to reshoot some scenes and do some voiceovers, but other than that, I should have about three months before I have to do my press tour."

"Looks like we are both going to be busy," I added, wishing I could find a way to spend more time with her. Our tour would start about that time, too.

"Oh, I plan on making a few shows on this next tour," she told me with a huge smile. "Braxton promised me a sneak peek at the dates as soon as they are finalized."

"We won't know anything for at least another few weeks. We have to get this album out first." I slapped my credit card down on the tray with our bill and quickly handed it over to the waiter.

"I was going to pay my own," she scolded, narrowing her eyes. When she did that, her bottom lip pouted, and all I wanted to do was reach over and smooth it back into its normal position.

"I got it," I chuckled. "Remember, I'm going to be uber rich come tomorrow."

"Well, you do have a point there." She smiled while giving her head a little shake.

Talking to Penny was so easy. She understood my past history with drugs and alcohol, and I didn't have to tread lightly with her. She had a sharp tongue and a wit about her that I liked.

"Let's head out," I suggested, standing from my seat. "You need your sleep, and I need to get up early, too. My meeting with the lawyer is at nine."

She allowed me to pull back her chair and accepted my hand as I helped her up. Five years ago, I wouldn't have been so chivalrous. The women I kept at my side were sleezy, and I had no respect for them. They were nothing but a quick fuck, and they fed my darker side. The drugs made me into somebody I didn't like.

"Fuck," she whispered as we reached the door.

The moment I looked up, I mimicked her words, seeing ten photographers lining the sidewalk to the left of the door. The valet area was clear, but I didn't want to wait outside for them to bring the car around. Instead, I steered Penny over to a seat and approached the hostess station.

"Is there any way you can have my car brought

around without me going outside?" I asked the young girl. When she looked up, I saw the recognition in her eyes. She glanced over at Penny and nodded her head. "There is an alcove behind this wall if you'd like some privacy."

Apparently, this wasn't new to them. I handed her my ticket and headed toward Penny. "Let's wait in here."

"They find me a lot," she deadpanned like it was an everyday occurrence.

"Are they hounding you?" I asked, feeling my protective instincts fire every nerve in my body. It stopped me short for a minute, because I hadn't felt like that in a very long time.

"If I go out in public, they always find me," she shrugged. "Honestly, Cash, I'm used to it. It never fails. I'm sure employees at the places I visit are paid to snitch. It's part of the game in L.A. Don't let it get to you."

The hostess peeked her head around the corner to let us know the car was ready. I grabbed Penelope's hand, because I wasn't going to let those vultures separate us. She had a lot more experience with them than I did. Usually, I only had them bother me while we were on tour. Being in L.A. was going to test my patience.

"You ready?" Penny asked as she donned her

sunglasses. "Make a dash for the car and don't answer any of their questions. Keep your head down, too."

"I hate that you have to deal with this," I said, crossing a line I promised myself I would never cross with my drummer's sister. I stroked her cheek, stopping when my crooked forefinger reached the underside of her chin, giving it a little nudge so she would look up into my eyes. "Stay close to me until I get you safely into the car."

"Okay," she breathed, giving me a nod after I reluctantly let her go.

The moment we stepped out the door, the night's sky turned into flashes of bright light. The photographers shouted questions as we hurried toward my rental. I wrapped my arm around her shoulders, tucking her face into my chest. She didn't say a word and kept up with my fast pace. The twenty feet to the passenger side of my car felt like a mile.

*Penelope! Penelope!*

*Cash! Cash!*

*Are you two a couple now? Cash! Penelope! Can we get a picture of you together?*

I knew they'd take our appearance together as something it wasn't. Knowing how fragile Penny was about her image in Hollywood, I wanted to protect her from their words, and thank god they didn't comment on her weight. She didn't need to relapse.

I waited until she was settled to shut the door, then grabbed the keys from the valet and handed him another tip as I was getting in. Three photographers lunged in front of the car as I started to pull away from the curb. With a curse, I hit the brakes, but the kid in valet saved me by pushing them back so we could leave.

"Well, that didn't go as I'd hoped," Penny chuckled from her seat. She removed her glasses and hat the moment we were safely away, dropping them into her bag.

"That's crazy," I breathed. "Fuck."

"You get used to it," she shrugged.

"Does that happen often?" I inquired.

"Only about ninety percent of the time," she replied and leaned her head back. "Let me give you the address to the house I'm staying at." I handed her my phone so she could pull up the directions on the app and plug it into the car's navigation system. I followed the screen prompts and got back on the interstate. I hated leaving her alone, but we both needed our sleep.

"So, I'll text you tomorrow after I meet with the lawyer," I offered as we reached her place. The house was bigger than my own. The white two-story home was lit by landscaping lights that pointed to the four pillars on the front. It looked like most older homes, but it was immaculately done up as if it'd recently been renovated.

"If I don't answer, I will send you a text when I get back to my dressing room," she promised. "Thank you for dinner, Cash. I'll talk to you tomorrow."

I watched as she keyed in a code to the garage door. Once she was inside, she gave me a little wave before closing me out. I didn't want to leave her, but it was for the best. Our picture together would be spread all over the internet in the next hour if it wasn't already there.

With a heated curse, I dialed Braxton to let him know before he saw it and wondered why we looked so damn cozy leaving the restaurant.

## Chapter 4
## Penny

My attraction to Cash only amplified after our dinner. We didn't flirt. We didn't touch in any way that should've caused me to be turned on by him, other than the way his hand felt against my lower back. What did it for me? The chivalry…the care he took with me as we rushed past the paparazzi. He didn't have to shield me, but he had.

Half of me thought it was because he cared for me more than just friends, and the other half thought it was simply because of my brother and his protectiveness. I knew damn well Braxton Keller had sent Cash to check on me, and with that, he felt obligated to hang out with me to make sure I wasn't doing anything stupid like sticking my finger down my throat again.

Having Cash at my side stirred a forgotten need. It'd been a long time since I'd had a connection with a man that brought out my secret desires. The last guy I saw was nothing more than a companion to fill my basic needs. He was a good man, but we eventually grew apart. We ended things amicably, and after that, my acting career started to take off. I'd landed a leading role in a movie that never even made it to the box office, and I focused on my acting and my family.

Braxton had been going through a lot during that time. Abby had come back into his life, and my brother was dealing with his past. I'd gone back to Seattle and helped him finally see how much he loved his ex-girlfriend. It'd taken some months of heartache before he had finally come to his senses.

Now, they were happily married and living in a nice house not far from our mother's place in Seattle. After their wedding, I'd put myself back out there, trying to find roles in other movies. Thankfully, the book that inspired the movie I was working on had hit the bestseller's list and was optioned to be made into a movie. It was fate that I looked just like the lead female character.

Giving up on trying to think over my attraction to Cash, I changed clothes and curled up in my bed with the remote. I didn't even remember settling on a channel to watch before falling asleep.

By the time my alarm went off, I'd had several dreams involving the bassist for my brother's band. It didn't help douse the flames of my desires, either. When my car arrived to take me to the studio, I'd filled my mind with thoughts of the scene we had to film for the day. I didn't tell Cash, but I would be making out with Malcom for the final scene.

The studio had been designed to look like my

character's home. He would show up and profess his love for my character, and the movie would end with them in a heated sex scene. We'd already filmed what was the epilogue in the book; a wedding. That had been a tough day with Malcom continuously complaining about having to kiss me.

I bet this sex scene would be the death of him.

As I arrived at the studio, my phone pinged with a text.

*Good luck today.*

I smiled at my phone, looking like a lovesick fool. Yes, I had a crush on him, but that was all it would be. Cash and I were compatible, but I doubted he was the type of guy who would give me the kink I desired.

*Keep your chin up at the lawyer's office today. It'll all work out, Ritchie Rich.*

He replied with a laughing emoji, then went silent. I would wait for his text to let me know how it went. I didn't want to pry, but I could tell he wasn't happy about revisiting his father's legacy.

"We're here, Ms. Keller," the driver announced as he exited the vehicle, coming around to the passenger side to open my door.

"Thank you." My voice was sweet. I locked down everything as I entered the door. There was a new security guard at the door, and he narrowed his dark brown eyes on my identification, looking between me and the photo twice to make sure I was who I said I was, and it made me want to laugh. He obviously didn't read the tabloids.

Speaking of tabloids, I pulled up one of them as soon as I entered my dressing room. My makeup and hair stylist was already there with my assistant, Terri.

"Let's get you ready." Terri was a temporary assistant. I knew I needed a permanent one, and my agent expressed his concern every single time we spoke on the phone. Once the movie came out, I would get one, but I didn't want to hire someone I didn't know.

The stylist got down to work, rolling and shaping my hair. I was too focused on the headlines to care what she was doing. Right there, on the front page, were the photos from our night out.

*"Breathless" star seen with Fatal Cross bassist, Cash Roberts.*

They didn't even have the decency to put my name in the headline. The next few articles were much of the same. They mentioned Cash's dad and my involvement in the movie of the decade. Of course, they speculated Cash and I were an item. We knew it would happen, but I was worried how my brother would respond.

I sent off a text to Braxton, telling him to stay off the internet because of the pictures. He had nothing to worry about, because we were only walking side by side with his hand on the small of my back until he tucked me against his side to shield me when they got closer. There were no compromising positions to make them twist and turn the headlines in their favor, even though they speculated a love affair.

Placing my phone on the makeup counter, I sat back and let them get me in character. Within an hour, Penelope Keller was transformed into Trinity Wells, bakery owner and the love interest of Caleb Gentry, former military guy who'd returned home after being in the war. He suffered from PTSD, but my character brought him back to life with her love.

It was sappy, but it was also a bestseller.

When I walked onto the set, I was blown away at the design team's work on the fake interior of my home. I'd read the book before we started filming, and I loved it. The couch, table, everything matched the book's description to a T.

"Last day, people!" someone yelled. I smiled as I

meandered through the set. The only part we'd be needing today was my living room and bedroom. Hopefully, Malcom would be in a good enough mood to get through this last part without his temper tantrums. Then, we could go on our merry way until it was time for the press tour. After it was all said and done, I would refuse to work with him. His negativity had no place in my life.

"Well, here we fucking go," Malcom scoffed the moment he arrived. He had two assistants, and they followed him around like the good little goblins they were. One held his script while the other handed him his coffee. The coffee holder was nothing but an end table. The man probably didn't even wipe his own ass. "Did they get you a body double?"

His question took me aback for a second. There was one thing most people didn't know about me unless they were in my inner circle. I really didn't take shit from assholes.

"I am the body double, you fuck," I sneered. "Either, we get this done on the first few takes, or you bitch and complain like a fucking pussy all day and we will have to come back tomorrow. Your choice…pick wisely."

I walked off. He'd already had my heartrate in dangerous territory. Why couldn't I just punch him?

I really wanted to punch him.

"Places everyone!" the director called out. She gave me a short nod, and I read over my lines one last time before setting the script in my chair. When the lights came up on the set, I worked my hardest to get the parts done to perfection. Thankfully, Malcom didn't complain much, and we were done before sundown.

After kissing him and pretending to fuck him for the better part of the day, I went directly to my dressing room and found my toothbrush. It didn't matter how much I scrubbed my teeth and tongue, I couldn't get him out of my mouth. That was the only part of acting I didn't like. I could handle most of the implied nude scenes because they dressed me in a bodysuit that matched my skin color.

*Can I pick you up tonight?*

Cash. Just seeing his text made everything I'd done that day disappear. He'd sent the message three hours prior, and that meant he must've been done with his lawyer.

*Come pick me up. I have to clean out my dressing room. We wrapped up filming today.*

He replied that he was only thirty or so minutes

from the studio, and I made use of the time, packing my bags. I ran my fingers over the dresses I wore on set, glad that part was over. I liked dressing up like any other woman, but I also liked my comfort. Now that filming was over, I could go back to Seattle and be myself again.

Cash had said he was leaving in the morning, and I looked online for the flight number he'd texted me. Thankfully, there were a few seats left on the flight. I booked it and set my phone down to zip my bag.

"Come in!" I called out when there was a knock on my door. When it opened, my heart skipped a beat as he entered. He'd left his blond hair down, and the locks were as long as my own. I wanted to touch them to see if they were as soft as I thought they'd be, but I resisted.

"All done?" he asked. His blue eyes sparkled as I smiled.

"Oh my god, yes!" I cheered. "Let's get the fuck out of here."

"Did you have any problems with douche nugget?" he asked, hitching his thumb over his shoulder to indicate he was talking about Malcom.

"When do I not have issues with him?" I scoffed, but shook my head when I noticed Cash's eyes darken. "Today went very well, but then again, I did tell him to shut the fuck up and get through these last scenes so we could leave."

"Good girl," he smirked. "I like your sharp tongue."

"Oh yeah?" I flirted, knowing what I'd like to do with my tongue. "You do?" *Damn it! Stop it, Penelope!*

"Totally," he winked, holding out his hand. "Let's get out of here."

Chapter 5
Cash

Penny and I boarded the plane from LAX to Seattle. We both wore our disguises, but it didn't do any good after the tabloids had splashed our photos across their front pages the day before. We'd signed several autographs before airport security caught on and moved the fans away to give us a few minutes of peace.

Once onboard, we talked to a man in first class who offered to trade seats with me so we could sit together for the three-hour flight. Penny had to give him a picture, but I didn't care as long as she was within my reach.

We had dinner the night before at her rental, because going out was just too risky. With the news of the movie building, she was going to be in the spotlight more than ever, and that worried me.

"Have you thought about hiring a bodyguard?" I asked once we were settled in our seats.

"I have," she nodded, but she looked away like she was hiding something. I gave her a moment to compose herself, then she looked up into my eyes. "How is that company you hired for tours working out?"

"They are top notch," I promised, reaching for

my phone. "I'll give you the number for Hayden Lewis, our head of security. He can get you a guy before you have to go on the press tour."

"I hate having to get a bodyguard," she said, sighing heavily. "Before you get all upset, I'm not saying I'm refusing to get one. I will…it's just weird having someone with me all the time."

"I know you're used to flying all over the place by yourself, but right now, you need to have someone around you that will protect you should something go down."

"Go down? Like a stalker?" She shivered when I nodded my head. The thought of a crazed fan getting his hands on Penny sent a chill up my spine.

"Shoot him a text now," I ordered. They were still loading coach, and we had at least ten minutes before they closed the door.

A flight attendant came by and offered us drinks. We both decided on a small water to get us by until it was time to take off. Penny sent the text before setting the phone on her tray table.

"Braxton would probably demand I hire someone, anyway," she said, rolling her beautiful blue eyes.

"He would," I nodded, remembering we were heading home. My time with Penny was about to come to a screeching halt. Returning to Seattle came with issues; her brother would be there, and I would be returning to my home out past Port Angeles. Any time we spent together would be when I returned to the city on Monday to work on the album.

"I'll be in town on Sunday night," I offered.

"That's four more nights," she wondered aloud. "Do you have a place to stay when you get in town?"

"I bought a condo close to the stadium and studio," I admitted as they made the announcement that they were closing the doors. "I stay there when I'm recording."

"That's a long drive out to your place," she observed. Penny had never been to my house, but she knew where I lived. The lake to the west of Port Angeles was beautiful and the peace I found there helped my anxiety and need for drugs.

"Almost three hours," I replied, wishing she was going home with me. "Would you like to come out for a few days? I have a spare room."

She tightened her fist on the top of the little table and looked over at me with darkened eyes. "Cash, you know what my brother would say."

"He wouldn't say anything," I smirked. "He'd just show up and kick my ass."

A bubble of laughter came out of her mouth, and I had to admit, it was contagious. By the time the plane pushed away from the gate, we'd both settled down. She was right, though. Braxton Keller would kick my ass if I laid a finger on her.

*But it would be worth it.*

"So, can I come out there tomorrow?" she asked, obviously not caring what her brother thought. In fact, she was right. Penelope was a grown woman, and if she wanted to spend time with me, Braxton really couldn't stop her. I mean, that big son of a bitch would try, but she would use her smartass mouth to get him off her back.

"You can come whenever you want, darling," I drawled, knowing I meant something entirely different.

"I might take you up on that offer," she blushed, unlocking her phone so she could go through her emails.

I tried my hardest not to look over at what she was reading, but when she stiffened beside me, my eyes immediately fell on a message from a fan. The time stamp said it was sent only five minutes before our flight was scheduled to take off.

"What the fuck, Penny?" I bellowed, snatching the phone from her grasp.

A man named Edward had sent an email, telling her how much he loved her and would see her when she landed in Seattle that evening. I read over the message twice before looking up into her wide eyes.

"Who is this?" Yeah, my temper and possessive side was showing, but at that point, I didn't give a fuck. This guy had creep written across his forehead in black ink.

*Hello, my love,*
*I will be waiting for you in baggage claim when you arrive tonight. I hope you have a wonderful flight.*
*Ed*

"I don't know," she sighed, waving her hand as if to disregard his email. "This guy has messaged me three times this week with the same email, claiming he was going to pick me up at the airport."

"And have you told anyone about it?" I pressed. Fuck yes, she needed a bodyguard, and the message on her phone was proof it needed to be done as soon as possible.

"No." She crinkled her nose, and I reached out to take her hand. Penny looked down at where we were joined and shook her head. "He's harmless."

"How do you know that?" I continued. "Penny, *this* is why you need a round the clock security team. You don't know this guy, and what if he's coming to the airport every day to see if you are arriving? He could hurt you…seriously hurt you."

"It's hard to see myself as a celebrity," she admitted. "You're right, though, Cash. I probably need to get someone as soon as we get to Seattle, but for the record, I don't think Ed is a problem. Look at the other emails he's sent."

She trusted me with her phone, and I scanned through the messages. There were four. Each one was a carbon copy of the one before; almost like he'd just copied and pasted the exact same thing into a new email and sent it.

"Thank god for Wi-Fi on the plane," I mumbled as I sent off a social media message to Hayden Lewis. He answered me right away, and I had Penny send me screenshots of the messages, showing the date and time stamps. "I need to know right this moment if you are willing to take on a security team, Penny."

"I mean, what all does that entail?" she gasped. "I have no idea what to do, Cash."

There was a slight bit of fear in her eyes, and I did what I do. Taking over for her, I typed out a message to Hayden, asking him to have someone meet us at the airport. The security guy would take her to her mother's house, and since it would only be dinnertime when we arrived, we could make plans to add on another man once she had to return to L.A. and started her press tour.

"Hayden is sending a guy from his team to meet

us as we come through security," I announced as I closed her phone and handed it over. "His name is Craig Huntley, and he will be waiting with a sign showing only my first name. He will get you to a waiting car while I pick up your bags. You and Craig will go to your house, and I will be there as soon as I can. My car is parked at the airport."

"Okay," she agreed. "Okay, Cash. I'm trusting you. This guy has never bothered me other than the emails, but I get it. I really do. My life is changing faster than my mind can process it."

"You're going to have some crazy men trying to meet you," I growled, not caring how possessive I sounded. "If you get weird messages, you are to forward them to Craig."

"So, just like that, you got me a team of security guards?" she asked. "I'm impressed, Cash Roberts."

"Well, I know a lot of people." I tried to play it off as teasing, but my dominant nature came through in the harshness of my words. "I think you should also message your brother. He's going to have a fucking fit if you show up with a bodyguard in tow."

"You're probably right." She cursed under her breath and sent the message.

## Chapter 6
## Penny

Okay, I was nervous as hell stepping off that plane, but Cash was there to guide me by placing his hand on my lower back just like he'd done before.

The hum of voices wasn't as soothing as usual. He'd gotten me so worked up about Ed, I was scanning the faces of every man that walked close to me. A few women giggled in the corner once they noticed who I was, and others were blatantly pointing at Cash as he walked with long strides to get out to Craig.

I had no idea what the man looked like until we passed through the exit line by security and a man wearing a dark blue suit approached us. He was super tall and built like a quarterback instead of a linebacker. I didn't know what type of strength he had behind his suit, but I was hoping it was enough to keep people from touching me.

"Ms. Keller? Mr. Roberts?" He flashed an employee ID and stuffed it back in his pocket when Cash relaxed. His short hair reminded me of a Marine, and his dark brown eyes matched what hair he had on the top of his head. The man was all business, and positioned himself to keep us from anyone's line of sight.

"Get her home, and I'll take care of our bags," Cash ordered. "I'll be right behind you."

Cash turned to me, and in a hurried rush, gave me instructions. "Stick with Craig and don't get separated. When I get to your house, we will go over a plan. I'll take care of your brother and call him as soon as I get our bags."

"Okay," I nodded, but my mouth was suddenly dry. Cash leaned down and kissed my cheek.

Voices around us alerted us that fans were starting to realize who we were. Cash looked around and narrowed his eyes at them. "Go. Get out of here."

"Ms. Keller." Craig said my name and moved to the left side of my body. I glanced at Cash as he hurried to baggage claim, leaving me alone with the guard. "Let's get out of here. My car is parked in the garage, but it's close to the elevators."

"Okay," I mumbled, looking around as the voices around me got louder. I felt a second of panic, but I didn't have time to dwell on it before Craig clasped my elbow and we were moving. "We need to go."

The moment we entered the elevator to get to the parking garage, I released a breath I didn't even know I was holding. "Fuck," I whispered.

"Everything is going to be okay," Craig promised as he straightened his suit jacket. He kept one button in place, and his tie never moved from its straight position.

"I know it is," I replied. "Cash was worried about this guy that'd been emailing me for the past few days."

"That's what I heard," he replied, pausing when the elevator reached our floor. "Come. We can discuss this in further detail once we reach your house."

Again, I nodded and let the man take me to his car, which really wasn't a car. It was a full-sized Escalade with dark tinted windows. He unlocked it as we approached and opened the rear passenger side door to help me inside. The cool leather seats felt great on my heated skin.

Craig rounded the vehicle and got us out of there as quickly as possible. I thought about texting Cash to make sure he had made it out of the airport okay, but didn't bother him. I had to trust he would call if he needed help. I knew they had security while on tour, but did they need it at home? Who was watching over him?

The drive to my house took less than thirty minutes. The moment we pulled into the driveway, my mother came out with a huge smile on her face, but it instantly died the moment she saw the strange man walking around the vehicle to open my door.

"Penelope? What's wrong?" Well, damn. My

mother used my full name, and that alone indicated she was concerned.

"Come inside, mom," I urged, looking over my shoulder at Craig. "We have a lot of things to discuss."

"Are you okay?" she asked as I walked over and pulled her into a hug. I'd missed her terribly.

"I'm perfectly fine," I promised, looping my arm through hers. I needed to sit her down and go over everything that had happened and what to expect once the movie premiered.

Craig walked over and introduced himself. "Mrs. Keller, my name is Craig Huntley, and I have been hired by your daughter. Like Penelope said, it's best if we sit down and go over everything inside."

"Okay," she replied, but there was still fear in her eyes. "Come on. I'll pour us some coffee."

It was after noon, but my mother's love of coffee didn't stop her from drinking it all day. Mom took her seat beside the head of the table, indicating Craig should take the head. That seat had been reserved for my dad. After he passed away, Braxton had taken over the spot at my mother's insistence.

"Mrs. Keller," Craig began, wrapping his hands around the coffee mug, but he didn't take a drink. "Cash Roberts contacted the company I work for in regards to hiring a security detail for your daughter.

She's received a few emails from a man named Ed that were of concern."

Craig removed his phone and pulled up the emails Cash had me forward to him. He slid the phone over to my mom to read. The longer she stared at them, the angrier she got. I could always tell when she went into momma bear mode from the thin line of her lips.

"Mom, he wasn't at the airport today," I said in a rush.

"Where's Cash?" she asked as she set the phone down.

"He should be here any minute," Craig replied. "He stayed behind to grab their luggage. His car was already parked at the airport."

"Okay, good," she sighed. "He's a good man."

"He is," I replied automatically. It was true. Cash Roberts was a gentleman. Every time we'd been together over the past few days, he'd gone out of his way to make sure I was treated like a queen.

I liked it, but my fantasies were running wild.

King in the streets and freak in the sheets was my saying. God, why was I thinking about him like that again? Braxton would kill us.

"Mr. Roberts is aware of the threat this man could be to Penelope," Craig continued. My hands were starting to sweat, and I took a sip of coffee just to have something to do with them. "I'd like to sit down with her and you to make a plan for everyone's safety. I know she is done with filming, but that doesn't mean she will be left alone. I've seen the tabloids, and I know the paparazzi will hunt her down to get any pictures of her they can."

"The movie is going to be huge, mom," I advised.

"That's wonderful for you, but I worry about crazy people coming here," she fretted.

"That's what I'm here for," Craig promised. "As we get closer to her press tour and release of the movie, I will bring in a team to help during the times she is away from the house."

"So, what do you propose?" I asked, but paused when I heard a car door close. When I started to stand, Craig held his hand out, stopping me from going to see who it was.

"First thing you're going to have to do is get over the normal routine you have," he began. "That door closing, although we know it's Cash, could be Ed or another person like Ed. From now on, I will answer the door or investigate anyone who comes on the property."

"Sorry, habit."

Cash entered shortly after, stopping to give my mom a hug and kiss on the cheek. He took a seat next to me at the table while my mother poured him a cup of coffee. My mind was reeling. There was so much I took for granted when I was home in Seattle. Like simply going to the store for groceries. I guessed that was a thing of the past now.

"My brother should probably be advised of Craig's presence," I blurted. "He's a big part of my life, too."

"Actually, I called him on my way back from the airport," Cash announced, giving me a side eye. "He's on his way now."

"Well, let me get some lunch started," my mom announced as she pushed back from the table. "There's no need to repeat everything, because I'm certain Braxton will be barging in here wanting to know anything and everything there is to know."

I chuckled as she shook her head. Mom wasn't oblivious to my brother's protective nature. He'd always been that way. He'd once gotten suspended from school when we were in ninth grade for punching a boy who'd grabbed my ass during lunch.

"Where would you like me to put your bag?" Cash asked as we all stood. Craig stayed at the head of the table to make some notes on his phone.

"I'll take it upstairs," I offered, but he narrowed his eyes.

"This thing weighs a ton," he teased. "Show me

where you want it, and I'll take it up there for you."

A little part of me felt like that high school girl again, knowing Cash Roberts would be going into my bedroom. I hurried ahead of him and opened the door to my room, pointing toward the bed. "Lay it up there. I'll unpack tonight."

My room felt smaller with Cash there. I could smell his unique cologne, and something about it had my body relaxing. His arms were strong enough to lift the bag without effort, and I watched the muscles tighten. I had to look away before I fantasized about him picking *me* up to toss me on the bed.

"I want you to listen to Craig," he stated, bringing me out of my daydream.

"I will," I promised. "It's going to take some getting used to while I'm home, because I'm used to driving myself places and going about my day as if I am a regular person."

"You're not a regular person anymore, Penny," he sighed. "You basically just won the lottery with this movie. Things are going to change, and they're going to change fast."

"I feel like they already have," I admitted, leaning my head back to stretch my muscles.

"Everything is going to be okay," he promised as I leveled my head and looked him right in his eyes. He'd kept his hair up in the ratted, black beanie, and I wanted to reach over and take it off his head so his long, blond hair would fall over his shoulders. But I didn't.

"My brother will be here soon," I sighed, reaching for his hand. When I squeezed his, Cash returned the gesture and pulled me closer. I licked my lips because they became instantly dry from the closeness. When he reached up to stroke my cheek with the back of his knuckle, I almost came undone right there in the middle of my room.

"I don't want anything to happen to you," he whispered, searching my eyes for something. I didn't know what he was thinking, but I didn't pull away. I liked being in his arms, even if we were only considered friends. There was no denying my attraction to him, and when he placed a kiss on my cheek, it only made me want him more. "Craig is one of their best. Listen to him and stay close when you have to go out of the house. The paparazzi will find you anywhere, Penelope."

I felt a sense of loss as he released me. I kept the sound of disappointment out of my voice. It really wasn't the best idea for the two of us to be in each other's arms when Braxton arrived, even if what we'd just done was harmless.

"Braxton's here!" My mom's yell up the stairs sent us moving. I made an excuse to go to the bathroom and sent Cash down to greet my brother.

Once I was in the bathroom, I locked the door and leaned against the counter so I could look at my face. With my hands fisted on the edge of the countertop, I made note of the blush at the tops of my cheeks. My skin betrayed me whenever I was aroused. There was no denying Cash brought out that part of me. If it wasn't so complicated with him being in my brother's band, I might've even pushed the issue of a romp beneath the sheets while we were in Los Angeles. God knows we'd been flirting for over a year.

By the time I came downstairs, everyone was sitting around the table. Braxton stood the moment I entered the room and took me into a tight, brotherly hug. "Jesus, Penny."

"I'm okay, Brax," I promised and patted his beefy shoulder. "This is just a precaution."

"Cash called me and told me about them following you," he admitted. "What happened exactly when you two were in Los Angeles?"

"They took photos of us leaving a restaurant the other night," I explained, fluttering my hand out like it was no big deal. I didn't need him getting pissed off for no reason. "They immediately speculated we were an item even though the pictures just showed Cash trying to get me to the car without being blinded by their damn cameras."

Braxton grunted and removed his phone from his pocket. I wasn't worried about what he would see online, because I'd spent an hour scouring the tabloids to see what they'd used for images. None of them were scandalous. It really looked like two people having dinner.

"I hate you had to go through that, Penny," he replied after he'd gone through several of the images. "So, you have a security detail now?"

"Yes, Cash referred me," I nodded. "We were just starting to discuss a plan, but waited until you got here."

"Well, Craig," my ever-intimidating brother began. "What do you have planned to keep my sister safe?"

Craig tossed out the basic security steps like staying close, letting him make any appointments that needed to be made, coming up with a route should we be traveling, and making a list of approved visitors at the house.

The entire time, my mother sat there with a shocked expression on her face. I felt bad because we'd just dumped all of that on her lap. It might be best if I found my own place to live. I didn't want to bring any of this to her doorstep.

"Mom, I'm worried about the house," I stated

once Craig had gone over everything. "I don't want them coming here and disrupting you."

"It's scary," she agreed with a nod. "But I want you to be here. I can abide by Craig's rules until your popularity calms, Penny. It's going to be okay."

I sure hoped so. I had the money to move into my own place, but ever since my father died, I felt like I needed to be with her. She'd taken his death very hard, and my mom wasn't one to enjoy being alone.

Cash sat forward in his seat, resting his forearms on the table. He cleared his throat, gaining my attention. When I looked up, he had a hard set to his jaw. I wanted to ask him what he was thinking, but I didn't need to wait. He blurted his offer, and that was when I saw my brother's head swivel dangerously slow toward both of us.

"Penny, why don't you come stay with me? No one will find you there, and I have plenty of room."

## Chapter 7
## Cash

*Well, fuck...*

I should've kept my mouth shut. The look Braxton gave me was full of ice and warning.

"I don't think so," he grunted. "She can come stay with us."

"She can do whatever she wants, because she is sitting right here," Penny barked. My cock twitched in my jeans at her words, but thankfully, I was seated where no one could see my reaction.

As much as I loved taking care of a woman, nothing made me hornier than a strong, independent woman who wasn't afraid to stand up for herself.

"You can decide what you want to do," Craig interrupted, playing the peacekeeper. "We need to go over your tentative press tour schedule before anything else."

Penny nailed her brother and myself with a hard glare before pulling out her phone to get the dates for Craig. He took the information from her and started making notes in his phone. "You have three months off before you are set to do your first interview in Los Angeles."

"I'm sure I'll be recalled to reshoot some scenes or do some voiceovers in the next week or two," she supplied. "Those shouldn't take but a few days at most."

While Craig and Penny worked on her schedule, Braxton jerked his chin to the side, indicating he wanted to talk to me in private. We hadn't talked much since I left for Los Angeles, and if he wasn't going to kick my ass for offering Penny a place to stay, I was certain he wanted information on why she was so distant with him.

"What was going on with Penny when you got to L.A.?" he asked, and I breathed a sigh of relief he didn't lay my ass out.

"Her co-star is a complete asshole," I cursed, clenching my fists. "He liked to cut her down and remind her that she wasn't a size zero. The guy is the biggest douchebag I think I've ever met, and I didn't even meet him in person."

"That motherfucker," Braxton snarled. "How did she handle it? Was she eating right? Did she go to the bathroom after you two had dinner?"

"Woah." I stopped him, holding out my hands. "Braxton, she's fine. I was actually worried for her, but she told me she had allies at the studio; one being her director. They reminded Malcom that Penny was the perfect person to play the character for the part. It pissed him off, but they got the movie done."

"So, she's okay?" he asked, needing a little bit of

reassurance.

"I know you worry about her, but I don't see her relapsing," I noted, leaning against the garage wall. "She really does have her shit together."

"Good," he nodded. Braxton's shoulders sagged with relief. "We have to be back in the studio tomorrow, and I don't want to have to worry about her. I'm glad you talked her into hiring Craig."

"I know you don't like the idea of her staying around me, and I get it," I replied, knowing I needed to plead my case to him about her staying at my place. "I've lived a rough life, but I've changed. Hell, we all have, but I have a condo here she can use, and if she needs to get away…far away, she can stay at my house in Port Angeles. No one will find her there."

"You make a valid point," he grunted, but I could tell he didn't like it. Abby had changed Braxton since she had come back into his life. If this had happened two or three years ago, he would've punched me and told me not to be sniffing around his sister. Now, he was suddenly agreeable and not such an asshole when it came to Penny. "Obviously, she is going to have to make the decision. As much as we want to protect her, she's stubborn, and she will decide what she wants to do for her safety. I just hope Craig knows what he's getting himself into."

"I think the scare with Ed made Penny look deeper into her safety," I admitted. "She's been nothing but understanding and accepting of the security detail, so far."

"Don't fuck with her head, Cash," he warned, but there was no venom behind his words. "She's been through enough."

"I know, Braxton." I stuck my hand out as a gesture of peace. He took the offering and returned the handshake.

I felt like I was living in some weird storyland when Braxton calmed enough to not yell at me for offering my home to his sister. The change in her status must've scared him.

He'd already been working with the company Craig came from with our tour. We had to hire a few bodyguards during the last one because of some crazed fans. It made everyone feel a little safer.

When we returned to the kitchen, Craig was standing there, looking out the back door. "What did she decide?"

"You said you have a condo here in Seattle?" he asked.

"Yeah," I nodded. "It's over by the stadium, and it's on the twelfth floor. Do you want to take Penny over to look at it?" I was a little shocked he'd brought it up. Penny had been living with her mother ever since their father passed, and I assumed she didn't want to leave because of that.

"I think I should go by myself first," he agreed. "It's safer if I check it out without her there. I need to make a plan should word get out where she is staying."

"That makes sense," I agreed and removed the key from my pocket, handing it over. "We will stay here with her while you go over and check it out."

"I won't be gone long," he assured me. "Penny wants to stay close to her mom, but she doesn't want the paparazzi coming here. This might keep people away from the house." I saw him glance at the elder female. She was in her late fifties, and by no means was she unhealthy or frail, but out of respect, it was for the best Penny take precautions.

Craig interrupted the women, excusing himself to go check out my condo. It wasn't much, but it would do. There was a doorman and they had tight security around the place. I gave Craig the information and address, promising to stay at the house with her until he returned.

"So, I guess I'm staying at your condo," Penny said as she left her mom talking to Braxton. Her brother explained everything, and Mrs. Keller understood the concern.

"Yeah," I said. "It's pretty basic, but it's

furnished. You have everything you need there, and I had someone stock it with food for me yesterday since I'll be in town for the next week or so to finish up the album."

"That would be nice," she sighed, not commenting on the fact that I would be staying there, too. "I can't even shop for myself anymore, huh?"

"Unfortunately, no," I replied. "After the success of the movie dies down, you might be able to have a taste of normal again."

"Ahhh," she blushed. "About that…"

"What now, Penny?" I asked, narrowing my eyes.

She walked over to her bag and removed an envelope. I'd seen it in her dressing room, but hadn't thought anything about it. Braxton looked over and made a move to stand as she walked toward the living room. I was a little confused at what was going on, but she didn't leave us hanging for long.

"So, I received this today, and I could totally get fired and sued for telling you this." She paused, removing a packet of paper from the folder. "The book this movie was adapted from is a three-part series, and with the popularity of the first movie, they have signed me to play the role in the next two."

"Oh my," her mother breathed out, letting it sink in. Mrs. Keller jumped from her seat the moment it all registered. "Oh my God! Penelope!"

"I know, right?" she beamed.

Braxton picked her up in a brotherly hug, spinning his sister around. "Holy shit, Penny! This is life changing."

They celebrated as a family, and I was so fucking proud of her. She'd had some small roles in low budget movies over the years. This movie deal was going to shoot her into A-list status.

"This is really great news, Penny," I cheered, giving her a sideways hug. I didn't want to hug her the way I'd done while we were in L.A. In California, I was able to use my entire body to press her curves against me. She probably felt my hard cock against her stomach, but I didn't care. Here, I had to care, because even though Braxton wasn't being an asshole about us flirting, he could turn into an asshole really quick.

Especially, if I came out of hugging his sister with a hard on.

Braxton and I shared a look, knowing Penny was going to be thrust into stardom. If she kept her level head, she would be fine. If people like Malcom got their way, they would destroy her. While her intentions of making a career out of acting were good, the results of their bullying could be fatal.

Chapter 8
Penny

It was getting late, and mom decided to go on to bed, asking us to lock up the house when we left. Braxton pulled me aside as Cash was busy with a few emails from the record label.

"Are you okay?" he grunted. I could tell he was fighting the need to say something about me staying at Cash's place.

"I'm fine," I replied, wrapping him up in a hug. Like usual, he melted into my embrace. I knew he loved me, and I loved him just the same. I laid my head on his shoulder. "Brax, I'm in a really good place right now, and I'm finally living my dream. Having to deal with Malcom for another movie is going to be a pain in my ass, but I will be okay."

"If he doesn't get his attitude adjusted, I swear to Christ, Penny," he paused. I knew Cash was going to give him the details of what he'd heard and seen at the studio.

"I can handle him," I vowed as I released him and leaned against the kitchen counter. I could see Cash over Braxton's shoulder, and he would occasionally glance at me. "Yes, he makes me angry, and yes, his opinion of me did get to me a little, but I'm a lot stronger than I was."

"I'm so fucking proud of you, though," he admitted, and it made me smile.

"We both have a lot of things to be proud of, Braxton," I reminded him.

"You're right," he agreed. He caught me glancing at Cash and looked over his shoulder. "You really do like him, don't you?"

"We haven't done anything, Braxton," I promised. "He's been nothing but a gentleman since he got to Los Angeles."

"He better be like that with you all the time," he warned, narrowing his eyes. "Look, he's been through a lot, too."

"I know," I sighed, placing my hand on his shoulder. "Look, Braxton. You need to let me make my own decisions when it comes to Cash. I'm not going to lie and tell you that I don't like him, because I do. We are friends, and he's really helped me out over the past few days. I would've been lost without his assistance in getting Craig there so fast."

"Just be careful, Penny," he reminded me.

Just then, Craig entered from the garage. He waited for everyone to gather in the living room before giving the okay for me to stay at the condo.

"There's room for everyone to stay?" I asked, knowing Craig wouldn't want to leave my side, and Cash had to be there because they needed to finish the album.

"Yes," Craig nodded. "I've spoken with security at the building, and they are prepared if word does get out that you're staying there. We have access to the parking garage and two locations in the rear of the building to come and go. You won't have to use the front entrance."

"Well, I guess we should get going," I replied. "Let me grab some things from my room."

Craig and Cash stayed in the living room while I ran upstairs to my room. I'd lived with my mom since my father died and I'd come out of the program to treat my bulimia. I wasn't ashamed of myself anymore, and since I'd learned to eat healthy and stay active, it made me not want to purge everything I put into my stomach.

The anxiety part of it was under control with medications, now. I had developed some medical problems as a result of my long-term purging. Ever since I learned to eat properly, my stomach ulcers had healed themselves, but I still had issues with irregular cycles. Tack on my migraine headaches, and it led me to a life of doctor visits, medications, and birth control to regulate my periods.

I double checked my medication supply, making a note in my calendar to get a doctor's appointment set up in three weeks for new prescriptions. I filled my second suitcase with everything I would need for a month at Cash's and set it on the floor. I scribbled a note on a piece of paper, telling my mom to call me tomorrow, and slipped it under her door.

As I reached the top of the stairs, I hoisted the suitcase up, grunting when I realized it was super heavy. Cash looked up from his phone and noticed me struggling. I gave him an exasperated sigh, blowing my bangs out of my face. "A little help?"

"Jesus, what are you bringing?" he teased as he took my bag.

"A month's supply of everything," I chuckled and held out my hand for him to go on down the stairs. He knew I was returning the teasing and just shook his head.

"I'll meet you and Craig in the parking garage," he said once we loaded the car.

"See you then," I said with a wave.

Craig opened the back door for me and waited until I was seated to shut me in. Once he was in the driver's seat, he backed out and followed Cash to his condo.

"Now that we are away from your brother and Cash," he began, watching me through the rearview mirror while simultaneously watching the road. "How bad is the bullying from Malcom? And have you received anything else from this man, Ed?"

"Malcom is an asshole," I admitted. "He's just a stuck-up, A-list actor. I can handle him most days, and if it wasn't for my director, I'd have knocked his teeth out a few times by now."

"What about Ed?"

I dug in my purse for my phone and opened up the email app. I scrolled through several spam emails and stopped when I found an unread one from him about the time we landed in Seattle.

"He emailed me about the time we landed in Seattle," I announced. "He just wanted to know where I was. Nothing else."

"Can you forward that recent email to me?" Craig asked, rambling off his company email. I did as he asked, dropping my phone back in my purse as soon as I was done.

"This sucks," I groaned and leaned my head back against the seat. Craig didn't respond, and I took that as a sign he was going to give me some silence. I didn't really want to get into it with anyone this late at night. The last thing I needed to do was let my mind wander about the crazy fan or my idiot co-star.

As we exited I-5, I watched as the street lights passed us by. Cash said his condo was downtown, but I didn't realize it was in one of the newer, upscale buildings by Pike Place Market. I always loved going to the market, but I hadn't been in a few years because I was always traveling for jobs.

"We're here," Craig announced as he turned into the parking garage. Cash was just ahead of us in his black Audi. My new security guard pulled the black SUV beside Cash's car and killed the engine.

Cash opened the door for me while Craig climbed out of the front. I slid out and grabbed my purse. "So, this is my new home for a while, huh?"

"You'll love the views," Cash winked. He'd pulled his long, blond hair up into a manbun since he'd left my mom's house. It uncovered his face, and I had to look away or I'd have been caught staring at him. He really was a beautiful man.

Cash waved a card in front of the door to access the building, holding the door open for me to go first. I took the rolling suitcase from Cash and made my way to the elevator with Craig taking the lead.

At the twelfth floor, we turned right and stopped in front of his condo. He waved the card again and pushed open the door. A small foyer with white marble floors made way into a large, open living room. From where I was standing, I could see a wall of windows, but I couldn't make out what was beyond them because it was almost one in the morning.

"Bedrooms are this way," Cash said, turning to his left. I followed him until he stopped in front of a closed door. "This is Craig's room. He wanted to be between us and the front door."

"Thank you." He nodded and left us to set his bag down on the bed. He didn't return, and I was certain he was okay with me being on my own since we were in the condo.

"My room is here," Cash said, pushing open the double doors at the end of the hallway, but he didn't go inside. "Your room is right here."

When he opened the door, I immediately fell in love with the place. Everything inside was modern with furniture like I'd once seen at IKEA. All of the countertops were white to match the floors, and the cabinets were a grayish brown. The bed was covered in a fluffy white comforter with several pillows against the plush, gray leather headboard.

I covered a yawn behind my hand as Cash rolled my bag toward the closet. He pointed to a door across from the bed. "There is a bathroom attached to your room to give you some privacy."

"Thank you, Cash," I replied. "I don't know how to repay you for all you've done for me since coming to L.A."

"No need to thank me," he promised. "Get some sleep, and tomorrow, you can relax."

"Does this building have a gym?" I asked, wanting to keep him in my room just a little longer.

"A pool?"

"If you want to work out, there is a gym and pool on the eighteenth floor," he replied, coming over to take me into his arms. "I want you to feel at home here."

"I think I'll be okay," I assured him.

"I have to be at the studio at ten tomorrow," he announced. "I don't know how long I'll be, but there is food in the kitchen, and you are welcome to it all. I know you have a special diet, and you can make a list for the store. I'll leave the number for Hilda. You can call her and she will bring whatever you need."

"Hilda?" I asked.

"She keeps the place stocked and cleaned for me while I'm here. Otherwise, she'd be at my house in Port Angeles," he stated. "You'll like her. She's super sweet."

"Okay, thanks." I yawned again. My mind was starting to mull over other questions I needed to ask him, but my eyes weren't cooperating.

"You're tired," he said, leaning down to kiss my cheek again. "Sleep well, Penelope."

## Chapter 9
## Cash

My mind was too busy to rest. Penny had placed all of her trust in me, and the dominant part of my mind was satisfied she wasn't putting up a fuss about her security. I wanted to care for her, but there was more to it than just that.

I shouldn't have kissed her cheek, because doing so put her scent on my lips. The perfume she wore was a fucking pheromone that made my cock hard. I was trying to be a gentleman with her, but all I wanted to do was bring her to my room and bury myself deep inside her body. *Jesus!* The fact that she was in need of protection was getting under my skin.

I had a dark side, and to be honest, her brother was right to warn me about touching her over the past few years. He knew a little about my previous women, but what he didn't know was that they were a means to an end…just pointless fucks to give me release. Oh, I liked to play with them, and found more than a few in those days who liked to submit to me.

Penny was different. I wanted to care for her as much as I wanted to tie her to my bed so I could eat her pussy until she passed out from the pleasure. As much as I wanted to go back to her room, I finally closed my eyes and slept for a few hours, waking up well before my alarm.

When I entered the kitchen, Hilda was already there, pouring a cup of coffee for Craig, who was already awake and working on his iPad. She was a little thing, but she was always up for taking care of me, making sure there wasn't a speck of dust in either of my houses. "Morning."

"Good morning," I replied and walked over to pour myself a cup of coffee before turning toward Hilda. "You didn't have to come so early today."

"It's all right," she replied, wiping her hands on the apron she wore religiously. Hilda had come recommended by one of the men who lived in the building when I purchased my condo last year. She'd just lost her job with another family who'd decided to move overseas. Hilda didn't want to leave her grandkids and resigned. She'd been a huge help to me since I traveled all of the time. Now that I had acquired my father's fortune, I was going to give her a raise and a nice little vacation as a thank you. "I needed to get groceries for you and your guests, anyway."

"Is Penny awake yet?" I asked Craig.

"No," he said as he shook his head.

Knowing Penny had a special diet, I used my phone to find some recipes she might like. "Hilda, do you know anything about a pescatarian diet?"

"Oh, yes," she said. "The daughter of my last employer was on that diet. I know a lot of recipes."

"Good, because Ms. Keller only eats that way, and I want her to have that available here," I replied.

"You don't worry about a thing, Mr. Roberts," she winked. "I know just the thing."

She excused herself and left Craig and I alone. I took a seat across from him at the kitchen table, looking out the wall of windows overlooking Elliot's Bay. "So, have you learned anything about this guy that's been emailing Penny?"

"No," Craig frowned. "I have a cop friend helping me search for him."

"I don't like her being alone," I admitted, feeling my protective side stir. "She'd been going all over Los Angeles without anyone watching over her for the past few months. From what she told me, the tabloids were hounding her more and more as they got closer to the end of filming."

"Fuck," Craig cursed. "I don't know how she dealt with them. I've had my fair share of run ins with the media with my past clients. They're assholes."

"They are," I agreed and drained my cup of coffee. "Do you think she will need more security once the movie is out?"

"Probably," he nodded. "Cash, it's easy to run security for rock bands. They don't go out into the stadiums and mingle with the fans. Any meet and greets you do are centered in one location. Penny, she will be paraded around the media. If she has interviews at news stations, fans always line up, and she will have to walk through a crowd, signing autographs and taking photos. I've seen it before so many times. Then there is the premier. They do a very good job of keeping the crowd controlled, but it can get sketchy if someone wants to get their hands on the actress."

"She's going to have haters and people who want to get close to her," I added. Craig needed to be told about Penny's past, but I wasn't going to be the one to tell him. She needed to do that today, and she needed to be open and honest with him so he could do his job to keep her safe, even if it was from herself.

"I'm going to make sure that doesn't happen," he promised.

"Thanks, man," I said as I stood from my seat. "Let me see if she's awake."

He went back to researching Ed on his iPad while I padded barefoot across the living room to reach the hallway. The door to her room opened, and a sleepy-eyed Penny came out with her hair in a messy bun, a tank top, and a pair of yoga pants that looked like they were specially made to fit her curves.

"Morning," she mumbled. "Coffee?"

"In the kitchen," I advised. "I was just coming to check on you."

"I'm good," she yawned. "I need coffee…then talk…m'kay?"

"Follow me," I chuckled. She obviously wasn't a morning person.

Once we reached the kitchen, I pointed to a seat at the table next to Craig. She hummed her agreement and sat down. I poured her coffee and grabbed the cream and sugar, setting all of them in front of her.

"Just black," she mumbled again, skipping on the additives. "Cream and sugar are not good for me. Well, neither is the coffee for my migraines, but I can't give it up."

Craig looked up from his device and glanced at me before leveling his eyes on Penny. "You have migraines?"

"Yeah," she sighed. "That's why I watch what I put into my body. Plus, I have some other medical problems, too."

"Like?" I pressed, unaware she wasn't healthy.

"Coffee first," she reminded me, taking a sip. "Give me ten minutes."

I took my seat at the head of the table, looking out over the water. My condo had amazing views of the Seattle Wheel. I loved the place, but I liked my home in the woods better. It was quieter. A part of me wondered if Penny would like it out there, too.

"I guess you should know everything," she finally said once the coffee woke her up enough to hold a conversation. I thought she looked sexy as fuck all rumpled from her slumber.

"What do I need to know, Ms. Keller?" Craig asked, setting his iPad to the side so he could give her his undivided attention. When I'd called our security guy, Hayden, asking for references, he'd immediately given me Craig's information. He was a seasoned security professional who'd worked for a lot of big name celebrities.

"Well, I guess let's start with the fact that I suffered from bulimia from the time I was sixteen until about four years ago." She was my age; twenty-eight.

## Chapter 10
## Penny

I spent the better part of an hour telling Craig about my journey to get myself back into shape after spending about eight years of my life purging everything I ate. It caused a few medical issues, and I laid it all out on the line for him. Cash was there, and I didn't even think he knew all of the bullshit I'd caused by using bulimia to help me stay thin.

"So, you take medicine for the migraines," Craig noted on his iPad. "I'm only taking notes, because I have to keep your health safe, too. If you are on any medications, I need a list of them, along with the times you are instructed to take them. Also, I need your physician's information."

"Sure," I agreed. "I can get all of that for you today."

"What about your heart and kidneys?" he asked, surprising me that he knew some of the long-term effects of bulimia. I glanced over at Cash, and he looked…worried.

"My kidneys are fine, but I do have some issues with my heart. They are treated with medicine."

"What about depression and anxiety?" he continued. When I gave him a questioning look, he set his iPad to the side and turned in my direction. "I have dealt with this before with another client. She was still suffering from the illness, and we were able to get her help. I studied up on it during my time with her. So, while I know a lot about it, I may have questions."

"I don't have a problem telling you about my issues with it," I admitted honestly, watching Cash out of the corner of my eye. I didn't know how he would take the information I was giving out so freely. "I checked myself into a facility and stayed there until the doctors were satisfied that I'd recovered. I'd gotten so bad that I was passing out, and I started to look like I was dying. I'd had headshots done for my media packet, and once I saw them, it hit me that I had a problem. My poor mother helped me while she was worried over my brother who was also in a facility for a drug problem. I don't know how she did it."

"She loves you," Cash answered, giving me a soft smile. "She loves you both."

It made me sad Cash didn't have a parent in his life like Braxton and I did. He'd grown up in such a different world than we had. He'd fallen into the same crowd as my brother, and thankfully, he'd also gone through a treatment facility to keep him from killing himself by drinking and doing all kinds of drugs.

"I know," I nodded, turning back to Craig. I

really liked him, and while we still didn't know each other enough, I trusted Cash when he said this guy was one of the best. "Anyway, I will get a list of my medicines for you today."

"I'd like to go over your migraine and anxiety episodes, too," he continued. "I need to know what to look for so I can get you to a quiet place to take your meds, or if I need to evacuate you from wherever we are."

"I appreciate that, Craig," I sighed. "I really do."

Cash poured Craig another cup of coffee, and I declined a second one for myself. One was enough, and it gave me the energy I needed to start my day.

"As soon as Hilda gets back, I need to head to the studio," Cash announced as he set his cup in the sink. "I'm going to shower."

Craig made an excuse to head to his room, and it left me with Cash. He'd been wearing lounge pants and a soft, white undershirt that hugged his thick shoulders. I'd tried my hardest not to drool when I came out of my room earlier. If I hadn't been in need of coffee, I might've made a comment about it.

"I need to get my life together, too. Craig has given me homework," I teased and stood from the table. "What time will you be home later?"

"I have no idea," he shrugged. "Depends on what the producer needs from us today."

"Okay," I replied, trying not to sound disappointed.

"Hilda went shopping for you," he admitted as we headed toward our rooms. "I told her about your diet, and she said she had experience with it and knew exactly what to pick up. So, I'm trusting her."

"That's very sweet. I will have to thank her." I smiled up at Cash as we reached the doors to our rooms. "I'll see you before you leave."

"Look," he said, pausing me from opening my bedroom door. "If you want to come to the studio today, I'm sure it'll be okay with everyone."

"Actually, I'd like to just take today to relax," I assured him. "It's been a long few months."

"If you change your mind…" He let the statement hang.

"I'll call you if I get bored," I promised and slipped inside my room.

The shower was more needed than I had anticipated. When I got out of the shower, I fixed my hair and put on just a little bit of makeup. I had to check the local temperature on my weather app because I'd been away from home for so long. I'd gotten used to the sunshine and comfortable temperatures of California. Like I expected, it was going to be fifty degrees and partly cloudy. Not bad for a spring day in Washington state.

I gasped as I exited the bedroom, running into Cash as he was stepping outside of his own door. His hands immediately grasped my hips to steady me, and I felt his fingertips tighten as he pulled me close to his body. "You scared me."

"I'm sorry," he said, giving me that sexy smirk that made the women in the crowd swoon. I wasn't oblivious to his charm, either.

"Are you getting ready to leave?" I asked, changing the subject. Daydreaming about Cash Roberts wasn't something I needed to do today.

## Chapter 11
## Cash

I adjusted my seat, getting ready to record my bass parts for one last song. Ace had already finished his vocals, but he didn't leave the studio. Braxton and Taylor were already on their way home to see their wives.

It was nearing six, and I hadn't heard from Penny or Craig all day long. I wanted to check in on her, but I let her relax. She needed to go over her life with her new security guy and make a good connection with him since they were going to be side by side for the next several months.

She would start her press tour for the movie when we were taking off on our headlining summer tour in July. We'd gotten the tentative schedule today, and I wanted to compare it to hers as soon as she had her final schedule available.

It was getting harder and harder to be around her without showing my attraction. The two times I'd kissed her cheek had been my first show of affection. I did know that tonight, I would probably take it to the next level. I couldn't stop thinking about her pouty lips and what they would look like wrapped around my cock.

Wasn't that just fucked up? Thinking about your

drummer's sister that way?

"Okay, let's do this," Giles, our producer, announced.

I focused on the song, keeping Penny out of my mind as much as possible. I didn't fuck up my part, and thank fuck for that. Within an hour, we were wrapped up and sent on our way. It would take a few weeks before the songs were mastered and ready to go for an end of June release.

July first would be a new tour, and I couldn't wait to get back on the road, but there was a part of me that didn't want to leave Penny alone with those damned vultures. With this Ed guy sniffing around, it made my protective side twitch.

"How's Presley?" I asked my lead singer. Maybe he could give me some advice without me coming right out and asking him how he handled being away from her when she was on tour.

"Doing great," he replied. "They'll be home in two weeks, but since we are done with the album, I'll probably fly out to meet up with her in Chicago tomorrow."

"That's good," I nodded, lost in thoughts of how I could meet up with Penny during our own tour.

"Something on your mind?" he pressed as he slid his laptop into his backpack. I saw the worry in his eyes, and I shook my head to let him know I wasn't in a dark place. We all worried about each other relapsing, and we'd made a promise to each other that we would have each other's backs should we feel like getting high or drunk.

"Women," I chuckled and grabbed my own bag.

"Penny?" he guessed with a sigh. When I didn't answer, he stopped in the hallway leading out to the parking lot. "Dude, I get it. I really do. You two have been dancing around something for a while now."

"She's been busy," I admitted.

"Braxton filled me in on her new gig," he stated. "I'm happy for her, but I hear it's caused some stir in Hollywood."

"Yeah," I replied, hoisting my bag higher up on my shoulder. "The movie is going to be huge."

"Oh, I already know all about it," Ace laughed. "Presley has done nothing but binge read the books ever since they came out, and that's all she talks about. She can't wait to get home and talk to Penny about it. She wants all the behind the scenes information she can get."

"That's great," I chuckled. "You should have her call Penny anyway. She's going to be here for a couple of months before she has to head out on the press tour."

"When does that start?" he frowned.

"Right as we leave for tour." Hearing myself say

it out loud put a pain in the center of my chest.

"Oh, man," he replied with a shake of his head.

"Yeah," I grumbled. "I guess I better get on back. Call me when you get home, and be careful."

"Will do," he promised, but paused with his hand on the doorknob. "Hey, if you two are bored, and can get away, you should come to one of the shows. That might save me from having to endure her obsession about the movie. Ya know, like, bring the source right to her."

He was teasing, and I just laughed, slapping him on the back. "I don't know if she can talk about it, but I'll ask her if she wants to get away."

"Perfect."

We said our goodbyes and left the studio. Thankfully, it was only ten minutes from my condo. When I parked my car, I was relieved to see the SUV still parked in its spot.

I used my card to enter the condo, and immediately smelled food cooking. I dropped my bag on the couch and noticed her sitting at the small bar overlooking the kitchen. She turned around as I approached and a smile lit up her face.

"Hey," she said as I pulled out a barstool. "How did it go?"

"We finished," I announced. "Everything should be ready to go and up for preorder in a few weeks."

"Then tour?" she asked.

"Actually, yes," I smirked, pulling out my phone. I found the email from the label and slid it over to her. "Here are the tentative dates."

"Oh, I received my final press tour schedule today, too," she cheered. "Let me grab my phone and we can compare."

She hopped off the barstool as Craig was entering the kitchen. Hilda was busy making dinner, basically ignoring us. I knew better than to make small talk with her while she worked, because she usually shooed me out of the kitchen.

"How was she today?" I asked, lowering my voice.

"Good," he nodded. "We went over a lot of things. She read the book for the next movie and made a lot of notes after we found the gym and worked out for an hour. Other than that, it was quiet."

My shoulders sagged in relief as he grabbed a seat at the kitchen table behind us. I sensed her returning to the kitchen and turned around. My kitchen was open to the vast living room; only the breakfast bar created a separation between the two. Penny was barefoot as she walked across the marble floors. I glanced down at her soft pink toenails and my eyes had a mind of their own as they tracked up her body.

She was in perfect shape, and it killed me that Malcom and a lot of the tabloids had given her such a hard time after she'd gained back her weight. I'd seen the before and after pictures of her when they'd been blasted all over the internet when she had started filming. She didn't even look like the same person, and to be honest, she appeared sick and on the verge of death in the before pictures. I liked her much better the way she was now.

I had to quit thinking of her rounded hips and long, sexy legs. I was three inches over six feet, and she came up to my chin without her shoes on. The night we'd gone out, she wore heels, and we were almost evenly matched.

"Okay, I used your printer, I hope you don't mind," she announced as she placed a piece of paper on the counter.

"No, I don't mind at all," I replied and took the paper, setting it next to my phone. I studied the dates and cities, trying to memorize them. I had to trust Craig to keep her safe during the tour, but it was going to be hard.

"Oh, looks like New York is going to be a match," she beamed as she pulled a pen from behind her ear that I didn't even see through her long, brown hair. She made a little star next to the July tenth date.

"Dallas," I pointed out, waiting for her to make

another notation.

"Los Angeles," I chuckled. "We just can't get away from that place."

"No," she frowned. "We can't." Something changed in her eyes and she tucked her chin as she looked at the floor, and I took immediate notice.

"What's wrong with L.A., Penelope?"

"You always call me by my full name when you are worried or serious," she noted, turning in her seat.

"Are you going to answer me?" I pressed, my voice going deeper. Her bowed head jerked up to stare into my eyes like she'd been summoned.

"It'll be crazy that entire day and the day after your show," she sighed, pointing to her paper. "The premier is the next night."

"So, you're not going to be able to come to the show?" I was confused.

"I can, but do you think you can go with me to the premier?" she asked. "I'd really like you there."

"I don't see why I can't," I offered, checking my schedule. "I can make the premier, but I'll have to leave first thing the next morning to fly to San Diego. We have a show."

"You don't have to come if it's going to be too much," she said, but I saw the hint of disappointment in her eyes.

I didn't even pause when I reached for her chin,

gently pinching it between my thumb and forefinger. I gave it a little tug so she would look at me again. "I want to be there."

"Okay," she mumbled, her eyes darkening. "Thank you, Cash. It really means a lot to me."

She was worried about the media and Malcom. God, I hoped that motherfucker didn't make a scene at any of the stops on their press tour or at the premier itself.

"Dinner is done," Hilda announced, turning from the stove. She made a shooing motion with her hands. "Go, sit at the table."

"Yes, ma'am," I replied and took Penny's hand as she began to stand. "We will talk more about this tonight."

She froze for a moment and searched my eyes for something, but she finally released a deep breath and nodded. "I need to get my medicine from my room."

"Everything okay?" I asked.

"I'll be right back." She turned and headed toward her room as Craig put away his iPad.

"She's taking her anxiety meds," he informed me. "She has to take them in the evenings. It's a hard time of the day for her. Maybe that's something you two need to discuss in private."

"Thanks, man," I replied as I took my seat. Penny returned a moment later and sat down, accepting the plate from Hilda. She made her own plate and disappeared into the quarters reserved for her on the other side of the kitchen.

Penny placed a pill on her tongue and reached for her water. She set it down and picked up her fork, taking a bite of the flaky, baked salmon Hilda had made. Beside the fish was a mound of steamed vegetables. She'd made Craig and I the same meal, but we had a homemade roll added to ours.

"We usually get together to celebrate the end of recording an album," I announced. "Looks like Braxton is hosting this time."

"When is it?" Penny asked.

"Probably Friday night," I shrugged. It was only Monday, and we had the week to prepare. "That's usually when we do it."

"I'll call Abby after dinner and see what they need us to bring," she replied, taking another bite of her food. I tried my hardest not to watch her eat, still wondering if the diet she stuck to was good for her.

We fell into light conversation with Penny asking Craig about his life outside of security detail. He admitted he'd never been married, and he had no plans on settling down anytime soon. He was our age, twenty-eight, and had worked as an MP in the Army before getting out two years ago.

"I figured you for a Marine," Penny admitted,

pointing to the top of her head. "The haircut."

"Nope," he smirked. "Army is much cooler."

They bantered back and forth while we cleared the table, and just like usual, Hilda came into the kitchen to take over cleaning up the dishes.

I needed to talk to Penny about the medicine she took. Just like Craig, I wanted to know everything. Craig left to go to his room, and I made my way over to where Penny was leaning against the back of the couch, looking out into the night. Stepping up behind her, I rubbed the tops of her arms. "Everything okay?"

"It's good," she promised as she turned around. I refused to release her and repositioned my hands in the same spot to keep her close to me.

"Can we talk?" I asked. "I missed a lot of what you had to say to Craig today."

"Sure," she nodded. I dropped my hold on her and took her hand into mine, guiding her over to the couch. I had something I wanted to ask her, too. It had been brewing in my mind for a while now.

"Have you heard from Ed?" I asked as she settled in. We both turned toward each other, sitting cross-legged on the oversized piece of furniture.

"No, thankfully," she replied. "I guess I'm going to have to get used to it. Craig says this is only the beginning."

"I'm sure it is," I said. "It's the fucked up side to being in the public eye. I know you've heard some of the stories from Braxton about crazed fans."

"Oh yeah," she chuckled. "Quite a few."

"I bet," I replied, reaching up to touch a strand of her hair. I did it without thinking, but she didn't push me away, either. The freak in me wanted to savor the smell so I could recall it later when I jacked off to her scent in the shower.

"Cash?" she breathed. "What are we doing?"

"I don't know, Penelope," I whispered and moved my hand to brush her cheek with my thumb. The move brought us both closer as she leaned into my touch. "I feel very protective of you."

"I like it," she said, closing her eyes and nuzzling into my palm. She was a badass woman, and she had a sharp tongue that I loved, but this side to her…the softer side, it unmanned me.

"You worry me sometimes," I admitted, and used my crooked forefinger to bring her chin up again. Every time I did that, her eyes darkened, but not in a bad way. She was aroused, and I knew it. "Tell me what you told Craig today."

"Well, there was a lot." She heaved out a harsh breath. "I told him about my eating disorder, but that I was recovered. I haven't thought about doing it since I came out of therapy. The scare I had with my heart was enough to get me the help I needed."

"What's wrong with your heart?" I frowned. She'd mentioned it before, but I didn't know the extent of her health problems.

"I had a small heart attack when I was twenty-two from the strain the bulimia put on my heart. The doctors warned me about making myself throw up after the heart attack, and I ignored them. It wasn't until about a year and a half later that I saw myself in a tabloid about six months after my first movie. They did a side by side "before and after" image of me. I looked sick…like I was dying, Cash." She paused to touch my hand when I gasped. "It's not bad…nowhere near as bad as it could've been. I'm on a daily medicine to control my blood pressure, and it's working."

"Good." I nodded for her to continue, but she grasped my hands before she said anything else. Hearing that she'd had a heart attack at such a young age sent chills down my spine.

"I have anxiety," she admitted. "It's always been there, and I can't even pinpoint when I starting showing signs of it when I was younger. It fed a lot of my body issues and my bulimia. I take medicine in the evenings now to combat the worst of it. The times between dinner and bedtime are the hardest. Not saying the rest of the day isn't. I have moments when

I get overwhelmed. Hell, everyone does, but sometimes, I just can't stop the panic from happening."

"I understand," I replied. I saw it at the airport. She didn't have to even say anything to me about her anxiety when the fans started calling out her name. Her eyes told me everything. "What about your migraines?"

"Those damn things," she scoffed and rolled her eyes. "Those have been around just as long. The diet helps a lot, but sometimes there is nothing I can do to prevent them. They just happen."

"What about these scars?" I pressed, rubbing my finger over the back of her knuckles. Her skin was pale, but the silvery, round scars behind her knuckles were easy to see.

"That's from purging," she said, pulling her hand away. "My teeth would cut into my hand when I would make myself throw up."

"Don't ever be ashamed of them around me," I scolded, taking her hands back into mine.

She gave me a soft smile. "I really fucked up my health by doing it, too. I had so many problems over those eight years. Thankfully, I got my head out of my ass and got myself straight."

"You've been through a lot with this, and it should be a reminder that you are a survivor."

"Thank you for not judging me," she said softly. "God knows I've had enough of that."

"I would never judge you," I promised and cupped her jaw again. This side of Penny was vulnerable, and she was letting her guard down to tell me everything.

Raising up just a little, I pulled her face toward mine, pressing my lips to hers. It was sweet and innocent, but it was enough. She didn't pull away or deny me. Penelope accepted my affection and hummed softly as she leaned in.

Her hand landed on my shoulder, and I deepened the kiss, using my tongue to capture her bottom lip, giving it a little bite. She took my queue and opened her mouth for my assault. By the time we separated, we were both panting heavily, and my cock was hard…so fucking hard.

## Chapter 12
## Penny

Cash never kissed me again after I'd told him about my fucked up life. I didn't know what he was doing to me, but I couldn't stop thinking about him or that night on the couch. There was a need and a passion in his kiss I couldn't even explain. He'd accepted me for who I was, and he didn't even try to give me advice or tell me everything was going to be okay. I'd heard enough of that in my life that it made me sick.

Craig pulled out of the parking garage at Cash's condo. Cash had decided to stay there with us after Hilda had gone out to his home in Port Angeles to check on things. We'd been busy with our jobs since Monday, and my brother finally told everyone to come over to his and Abby's house for a celebratory cookout once we finally had a sunny day in Seattle.

The weather was still a little cool, and I dressed in layers just in case I got too cold. Braxton promised me he'd had Abby pick up some fish and veggies so I didn't get stuck eating a salad while everyone was gorging on steaks.

"What do you say about going out to my house next week?" Cash asked, bringing me out of my thoughts.

"Yeah, sure," I replied. "I'm almost done making notes in the book for the next movie." I'd taken the author's book and used color coded tabs to mark locations of importance to keep myself engrossed in the characters. "What do you have planned?"

"Nothing, really," he shrugged. "I just want to get out of the city."

"You don't like it here?" I frowned.

"It brings back too many bad memories," he admitted. I reached across the seat and took his hand. He tightened his hold on me and leaned his head back on the seat. "It's quiet and secluded out there. I miss it."

"I'd love to get away," I replied. "How close are you to some hiking?"

"Not far at all," he beamed. "Do you want to go, because I'd be down for a hike? I need to get back into shape before tour."

He did not need to get back into shape. The man was ripped and toned enough as it was. "I haven't been able to get away while I was in California. So, yes, let's do it."

"Craig?" Cash called up to the front seat.

"Sir?" Craig responded.

"Are you up for it?"

"Gladly," he nodded. It wasn't a hardship to find nature things to do in Washington State. There were mountains and rain forests everywhere.

"Let's plan on leaving Seattle Sunday," Cash announced, getting an agreement from us both.

When we arrived at my brother's house, Craig parked behind Taylor's car and held open my door while Cash came around to my side. We didn't hold hands, and even though my brother had backed off on the posturing, I didn't want to push it. He was too protective of me, but I still loved him. He'd taken the news hard when he found out I'd had a heart attack.

"Penny!" Abby yelled as I came in the house. We hadn't seen each other since I'd returned from Los Angeles, and I hugged her as tightly as I could. It felt so good to have some sense of normalcy in my life.

"I missed you," I said once we separated.

"Come on out back." She paused, looking over at Craig. "Is this your new bodyguard?"

"Craig, this is my drummer's wife, Abby," Cash introduced. They shook hands. "Come outside and I'll introduce you to everyone else."

Craig made his way out to the back deck and made the rounds. Cash broke off from us to talk to Taylor and Coraline, who was sitting in one of the chairs, holding their baby girl, April.

"How's the guy working out?" Braxton asked as he took me into a warm, brotherly hug.

"He's great," I promised. "I hope I don't need to

hire more."

"If you do, then get them," he ordered, narrowing his eyes. "Word has it that your movie is all the rage."

"The internet is going crazy," Coraline blurted. When I looked over at her and Taylor, he rolled his eyes.

"She's obsessed with the books," Taylor huffed. "Not liking her fantasizing about Malcom Sterling."

The thought made me cringe. "He's perfect for the roll, but don't worry, Taylor, he's a complete douchebag."

"Oh, great! Just ruin it, why don't ya." Coraline feigned hurt, before laughing at Taylor's scowl. "So, tell me, anyway. How close to the book is the movie?"

"You know I signed an NDA, right?" I warned, giving her a little wink. She could take that hint as she wanted, but my lips were sealed. She handed over her little girl and came over to give me a hug.

"I won't hold it against you," she whispered so the men around us couldn't hear. "But Malcom is still fine as hell."

She gave me a little finger wave and went inside, coming back with a glass of water. Taylor pulled her close as she took her seat. He was too engrossed in his daughter to say anything else about the movie.

"Do you want something to drink?" Cash asked

as he got up from his chair.

"Sure," I replied. "I'll go inside with you."

Braxton cut his eyes in our direction, but he didn't say anything when Cash put his hand on the small of my back as we walked inside. Abby passed us with an empty plate to take out to my brother and wagged her brows when Cash wasn't looking.

I leaned against the counter as he added ice to his cup. I took mine room temperature, and he nodded when I told him.

"Any word on when you will need to go back to Los Angeles?" he asked, setting his cup aside.

"Not yet," I answered. "I should hear from them by the end of next week."

"Have you told your brother that you are going with me to Port Angeles?" he asked, coming to stand in front of me. I didn't stand from my relaxed pose.

"No," I admitted. "It hasn't come up."

"Are you going to tell him?" he pressed.

"Maybe," I drawled, shrugging when he narrowed his eyes. "Probably."

"You should tell him, Penelope." There he went again, using my full name. I liked it when he did that. I liked the bit of dominance I heard in his voice. "Because we don't keep things from each other in this band, and if I take you to my other house and Braxton finds out we didn't tell him, he's going to show up out there. I don't think you want that."

"Why wouldn't I want my brother to show up at your house?" I was flirting with him, pushing him to kiss me again, and it worked.

"I wouldn't want him to show up unannounced while I had you in my room," he teased, capturing my lips for a heated kiss. He quickly stepped back and ran his gaze over my body. "Yeah, definitely don't want that to happen."

He picked up his glass and walked past me, giving me a sexy smirk as he left. That look alone caused an ache in my lower belly. I wanted nothing more than to give him my own kiss and beg him to touch me like I'd been dreaming about all fucking week.

As soon as he left the kitchen, I sagged against the counter. He hadn't outright flirted with me in over a year. The soft kisses to the cheek were just on the dirty side of friendly, and he'd been a gentleman. I wasn't complaining, far from it, but I liked it when he came on to me while we were in public. Call me crazy or call me weird, but it caused a wetness between my legs.

I straightened when I heard the back door open and close. Praying the blush had disappeared from my face, I busied myself with refilling my almost full glass and took a healthy sip.

"You okay in here?" Braxton asked as he entered with a plate of food.

"Yeah," I answered. It wasn't a lie, sort of. I still wanted Cash between my legs, but without his presence, it was easier to handle. "I need to talk to you before we leave tonight."

"About?" he asked.

"Ah, well," I stammered. "Cash and I are going to his house in Port Angeles for a week. He wants to get out of the city, and to be honest, Brax, so do I."

"Hm," he said as he set the plate on the counter, turning toward me while folding his arms over his chest. "I see."

"You see?" I asked, raising a brow. "What's that supposed to mean?"

"Is he good to you?" he growled.

"He's been the perfect host, Braxton. You have nothing to worry about." I was being honest with my brother. Cash Roberts may have been a manwhore in his former life, and maybe after it, but he treated me with respect. "We get along really well."

"Do you like him? And cut the friends crap, Penny. Do you have feelings for him?" Braxton could always read me like a book, and I never lied to him.

"I do," I agreed, walking over to wrap my arms around his big fucking shoulders. Where I'd gotten my thick thighs from my mother's side of the family,

Braxton got all the muscles from our father. We might have been twins, but we were nothing alike. "He's good to me, and he treats me well."

"I've had an ass chewing from Abby about leaving you two alone," he grumbled as I released him. I knew his wife could force him to see reason, but he didn't like it. "I've warned him away from you so many times over the years, but now, with him offering you a safe place to stay, I know it's going to happen. I just want you to be happy, Penny, and if Cash is the one to give you that, then so be it. My offer still stands, though. If he hurts you, I hurt him ten times worse."

"Okay," I chuckled. "I don't want you to have to do that."

"Just be happy, Penny," he continued, reaching for a stack of plates. "That's all I ask."

"Thank you, Brax," I replied, kissing his cheek. "I love you, big brother by six minutes."

"I love you, too," he grunted. "Now, go get everyone and let's eat before the food gets cold."

## Chapter 13
## Cash

The ride back to the condo took a little longer than expected due to a wreck on the interstate. Penny was beside me, looking out the window. She'd yawned a few times, and I reached for her hand, giving it a little tug so she would lean against my side. I stroked the side of her face and urged her to rest her head on my shoulder. "Take a nap. I'll wake you when we get home."

*Home.* Saying the word to her made it feel permanent…like she already held a residence there. I'd tried to keep her as safe as possible, because I cared for her. It was more than an attraction. I'd always thought she was stunning, but now that we'd gotten closer, I felt personally responsible to hold her against me to keep anyone from hurting her. I was quickly becoming obsessed with her.

My dominant side fed off of her need for protection, and it was killing me knowing I was going to be on tour while she was off on her press tour at the same time. I trusted Craig…I truly did. The company he worked for was one of the best in the business, but knowing I couldn't have my eyes on her worried me.

As we pulled into the parking garage at the

condo, I cupped her face and rubbed my thumb over her cheek, "We're here, babe. Wake up."

"Oh, sorry," she mumbled, blinking against the fluorescent lights of the garage. "I didn't mean to fall asleep."

"You were only out for a few minutes," I promised. "Let's get you inside."

She slowly got out of the SUV when Craig opened her door. I followed her out and took her hand as we approached the entrance. We didn't speak as we rode the elevator to the twelfth floor. Penny leaned against the back wall and blinked away her sleep. Craig left us at the door to go to his room once we were safely inside.

"Come, let me draw you a bath," I offered, wrapping my arm around her waist. She melted into my side and let me take her to my room. It wasn't much different than her guest room as far as the color scheme, but my room was about twice the size and my bed was bigger. I kept the windows covered with darkening curtains for those mornings that I needed to sleep in after long nights at the studio.

"Oh wow," she whispered as we entered the bathroom. "This tub is big enough for your entire band."

"Um, no. The guys and I would never be sharing a bath," I joked, releasing her so I could lean over and start the water. "I have a robe you can use after you are done. Take your time and head to your room. I'm going to be in the living room working on some social media posts."

"Thank you," she said as the steam from the hot water started to fog up the room. Her cheeks turned a little pink from the heat, and I had to get out of there, or I'd be asking to wash her back.

I closed the door and stood there for the longest time. She finally turned off the water, and I heard a soft moan. My forehead rested on the door, and I felt my cock harden. I didn't want to imagine what she looked like in the tub, and I pushed away with a soft curse.

I headed for my living room, and grabbed my laptop from the coffee table. I pulled up the band's social media accounts and got down to work, scheduling posts for the upcoming week. It was my job to keep them going, but I didn't mind doing it. I was fairly good at making graphics and videos to share. Some days, I spent hours answering questions and making comments on the sites. Tonight, I wasn't going to reply to many of them, but I did answer the ones that had been posted in the last two days.

I glanced up when I heard my bedroom door open. My cock instantly hardened the moment she came down the hallway still dressed in the white robe

I kept in the bathroom. She'd tied the sash around her waist, and I wanted nothing more than to pull her to me so I could yank it free.

"Thanks for the bath," she said, hiding a yawn behind her hand. "I just wanted to say goodnight."

"Goodnight, Penelope," I replied. "Get some sleep, and I'll see you in the morning."

"It's late," she frowned. "Aren't you going to bed?" It was late. A glance at the clock confirmed it was nearing one in the morning.

"I don't usually sleep until two or three," I said. "I have to schedule these posts for our social media. It's time to get the fans excited about the new album and tease about the tour."

"I need an assistant to do all of that for me," she frowned. "I have all of the sites, and they are steadily growing in followers. I just don't know what to post."

"I can give you some ideas, but why don't we do that in the morning?" I asked.

"Sounds great." She yawned again. "Goodnight."

Penny walked out of the room, her long hair swaying as she went. It took all of my strength to keep my ass planted on that couch. *Fuck my life.* I just wanted to tuck her into the bed. *Jesus. Fuck.*

We had tomorrow left in Seattle, and if she needed help with her social media accounts, then that was what we would do. Maybe it'd keep me from wanting to get lost between her legs.

No, it wouldn't.

I had to ignore the raging need to fuck her and get my work done before I did something stupid.

By the time I finished, it was well after two in the morning, and for once, I was tired. I stopped at her door and listened, satisfied when I didn't hear anything coming from the room. She was asleep, and I would do the same, knowing she was safe and sound.

I no more than closed my eyes before they opened and the clock on the side table said it was ten in the morning. Rolling onto my back, I laid there for the longest time, trying to calm my raging hard on. Penny was weaving her way into my dreams and every waking thought. I tossed the covers aside and looked down at the evidence of my thoughts, groaning when she came to mind again. I had to get my shit together or fuck her, because I didn't need to be walking into the kitchen with my dick hard and run into Craig and Hilda.

Instead, I jumped in the shower, letting the hot water run over the back of my neck as I put one hand on the tile and the other around my cock. It didn't matter how long I stroked, the pain of need only amplified. Her name sat on my tongue as I felt my body begin to tighten. Her beautiful face was in my mind's eye, and the visual of her body clung to my soul. I closed my eyes, willing the images to change to her underneath me, calling out my name as I coaxed every last ounce of pleasure from her body. With a groan, my release came, making my body sag from its strength.

We had only weeks left together before she went back to Los Angeles, and I would be preparing for a tour. We had so much to do in such a short amount of time, leaving me with one week at my home in Port Angeles. I couldn't imagine leaving her here, and I was relieved when she agreed to come with me.

Craig would be with us, but I had a pool house he could use for his own. I would have my house and Penelope to myself. I'd made a promise to her to help her with her social media, and today we would work, but tomorrow, we would start a short trip to decompress before the next phase in our careers began.

Dressed in a black t-shirt and gray sweats, I made my way into the kitchen, where I heard the coffee pot gurgling its last moments of brewing. Hilda reached for a cup and shooed me from her area. I chuckled as she poured my cup and handed it over. "I heard the shower and thought you'd like a fresh pot."

"Thank you, Hilda," I replied and took my first sip. Penny and Craig were gone, and I assumed they were in their respective rooms. "Where is everyone?"

"Ms. Keller asked to run over to her mother's home today to grab a few things. She and Craig left about an hour ago," she supplied. A bit of panic shot through my heart at her being out in public, but I had to not let it get to me. She wasn't mine, yet. I had no say on where she went or who she was with. The only thing that kept me from calling her was the fact that she'd had Craig take her to the house. Since they'd only been gone an hour, it wouldn't be too long before they returned.

"We are returning to the main house tomorrow," I reminded her. "If you'd like to go on in advance, we can take care of lunch and dinner here."

"If you're sure?" she fretted. I loved Hilda. She'd become a friend, and sometimes the mother I didn't have anymore.

"I'm sure," I promised. "Depending on how Craig feels about it, I may take Penny out to dinner tonight."

"You like her," Hilda said. Her weathered cheeks turned a little pink when I nodded. "She's a good girl, Cash."

"She is," I agreed. But I wanted her to be a bad girl in my bed.

"I'll clean up and pack my things," she stated, wiping her hands on her apron. "Leave your clothes by the door so I can get those washed at the house, too. If you could tell Ms. Keller and Mr. Huntley to do the same, I would appreciate it. I'll leave here at noon."

"Yes, ma'am." She left me sitting at the breakfast bar to head to her quarters. I finished my coffee and went to my room to brush my hair and teeth. When I returned, Penny and Craig were coming through the door with a small duffle bag.

"Sorry, we left without letting you know," she announced the moment I entered the living room.

"Hilda told me," I offered. "She asked for you both to gather your laundry and put it in the foyer. She will be heading to the house in Port Angeles at noon to get everything ready there."

"That's very sweet of her, but I can do my own," Penny offered.

"She loves to do it," I sighed, shaking my head a little. "Hilda will be upset if you do it. Trust me."

"Okay," Penny chuckled.

Craig started to leave, but I held up my hand to stop him. "I'd like for us to go out to dinner tonight. Do you think that would be a problem?"

"At this time, I think you will be okay," he admitted, straightening his suit coat. "As far as I know, the media doesn't know where she is."

"You research that?" Penny asked, her eyes wide

with wonder.

"It's my job to be two steps ahead of anyone or anything that can harm you. I search the tabloids and other websites several times a day to see what is being said about you."

"Wow," she breathed, then looked at me. "Can you still help me with my social media accounts?"

"Of course," I replied with a nod. "We can do a few things to keep the fans interested in the movie, and hopefully, the media satisfied enough to keep them from bothering you until closer to the movie's release."

"Do you think it's wise for us to be out in public tonight?" she asked, and I wondered how deep that question really went.

"Thank you, Craig," I said, not answering her until we were alone. "I'll decide on a place and send you the information."

He nodded and headed toward his room. Penny accepted my outstretched hand when I held it up, and I pulled her over to the couch. "Sit."

"What's wrong, Cash?" she asked.

"Are you worried about us being seen together? Is that why you asked that question?" I wasn't asking her because I was hurt or angry. My needs were for her.

"No," she promised. "It has nothing to do with

being seen with you. It has everything to do with us being portrayed as a couple. If that happens, they're going to dig up all that they can on you. I'm worried they'll scandalize your past like they've done mine."

"Everyone knows I was an alcoholic and addicted to drugs," I said with a shrug. "It doesn't matter to me, Penny. I don't really give a fuck what they say. I know who I am now."

It was true. They couldn't hurt me with their words, because I'd already dealt with my addictions, and thankfully, refused to go back to those days. It would've been easy to fall back into the habit over the years, but I had a great support system. There was no way I'd even look at a drink or line of coke again. It wasn't worth losing what I had.

"Okay," she replied with a smile, taking my hand. "I don't want them to say anything that might change things."

"I've done my time. I don't care if the stuff was free, I wouldn't touch it," I vowed. "I wasn't an emotional drinker or drug user. I did it because of the way it made me feel. I thought I was invincible. The alcohol kept the party going, and the cocaine kept me energized to be the life of it."

"I get it," she sighed. "I really do, Cash."

"Okay, enough about my past," I said, pulling her to her feet. "Get your laptop and head to the kitchen.

We have work to do."

"Yes, sir," she said and left. I took my computer from the coffee table and set it down on the breakfast bar to grab another cup of coffee. I didn't wait to ask her if she'd had one, because I knew she didn't drink but one a day. And after seeing her that first morning as she stumbled out of her room, I knew she'd already had one to wake herself up. Penelope wasn't a morning person.

## Chapter 14
## Penny

By early evening, I'd set up posts for all of my social media accounts. Cash had shown me how to use a program that would post across all of them at once. It would cut down on a lot of time. We would be free to just lounge at his house over the next week, and I couldn't wait to get away, maybe even go for a hike.

"Why don't we get ready to go out for dinner?" he asked as he closed his laptop.

"Sounds good," I replied and gathered my things. A look at the clock said we'd been working for a while, and I knew I should eat something soon. "Give me about twenty minutes."

"Take all the time you need," he urged. "I'll let Craig know we will be ready to leave in half an hour."

I hurried off to the bedroom to freshen up my makeup and grab something to wear. It was cold outside, and since the sun had set, I would need a jacket. I settled on a pair of black jeans, my tall leather boots, and a bright yellow blouse. Thankfully, I'd grabbed my thick, black pea coat before I'd left my mom's earlier in the day.

After redoing my makeup and curling my hair, I

added some hoop earrings and a bracelet to match before going to the living room to find Cash already there in his ripped up jeans and thin concert shirt. Somehow, the material laid just perfectly across his shoulders; the short sleeves protesting against his biceps. Beside him on the couch was his leather jacket.

"You look beautiful," he praised, leaning down to kiss my cheek. I really wanted him to stick his tongue down my throat and tell me he'd be eating *me* for dinner, but I smiled and turned toward my new bodyguard when he entered the room.

"Thank you," I whispered over my shoulder as we headed out the door.

Craig let Cash hold open my door and got inside to crank up the SUV. I'd had a good morning with Craig while I was visiting my mom. We got along well, and he had asked me a little more about my time in California. He was from the Seattle area, but he didn't have any family. It made me sad, but he reassured me that he loved what he did and wasn't looking for anything long term should he find a woman.

"You're quiet," Cash said at my side.

"For once," I chuckled. It felt good to get dressed up and go out on the town even if there was a chance I'd be photographed by a bunch of people. "I was just thinking about California."

"Let's not think about that until we have to," Cash suggested. "Tonight, we will have a nice dinner, and tomorrow, we head out to the house. After that, you have a week to just relax and be yourself. Soon enough, we will be working non-stop and will be glad we decompressed at my house."

"Good plan," I said with a nod, reaching for his hand. "Where are we going for dinner?"

"It's a surprise," he winked. I rolled my eyes and looked out the window. We were heading toward the water, and since there were several restaurants down there, I couldn't figure out where we were going.

I didn't have to wait long before Craig pulled us up to the front of an exclusive restaurant I'd not been to since they opened about a year ago. Cash waited for Craig to come around and open our door. He slid out first, then held out his hand to help me. His hand was warm against the cool evening air.

The building was an old, small warehouse painted white with weathered wood made into shutters. The double doors to enter the building matched, and a woman opened them as we approached. "Good evening."

"We have reservations for Huntley," Cash announced, casting a sideways glance at Craig. I didn't have to ask him why he had used Craig's name. My bodyguard had already informed me on the fact that all reservations would need to be made under an alias from now on. Not doing so could tip off photographers. They had people working in restaurants who would call in a celebrity sighting in a heartbeat.

The hostess showed us to a table in the back. The little alcove was perfect for our meal. Craig stood behind a chair on the side where he could watch the front of the building. Cash moved to the back of the alcove, and I sat to his right side. Craig nodded from across the table and took a seat.

Once the waitress came by and took our drink order, I searched the menu, knowing the place catered to different diets from the article I'd read on them back after they'd opened. My eyes widened with each selection. Almost everything on the menu was a part of my diet. They had several different options for seafood and even more selections for vegetables.

"Cash." I gasped softly, looking over at him. "This place is…perfect."

"I knew you'd like it," he replied. "I wanted to make sure your diet was covered."

My head bobbed in agreement, and I immediately looked at my menu, trying to decide what to eat. He'd thought of my needs, and I was shocked, but I should've known better. Cash had been nothing but accommodating since we'd left Los Angeles.

I ended up ordering risotto with spring vegetables and seared scallops. Craig ordered grilled salmon, and Cash decided on a sushi bowl. It made my heart soar that he'd brought me here. With my future about to explode, we should've stayed home, but it was obvious he wanted to do something special for me.

"Hilda is at the house already," Cash began. "She stopped and grabbed some groceries for the next few days, but she asked if you'd sit down with her and make a meal plan for the week."

"Me?" I asked.

"Yes, you," he chuckled. "We are men, Penny. We'll eat just about anything you put in front of us."

"Oh, okay," I replied. "I have a lot of recipes I've been wanting to try. I'll share those with her."

We were interrupted when our food came. The clinking of silverware took over our little hideaway as we ate in silence. Craig wasn't much of a talker, and he sat across from me enjoying his meal, but his eyes were on the crowd and the front windows of the building.

We eventually relaxed and sat there laughing and talking about the next week. "Craig, you are welcome to take some time off if you need. My home is secluded."

"Still not secluded enough," he chuckled. "I trust you, but I once had a client who lived in the mountains of Tennessee. He said no one could find him out there, but I decided to go with him. Good thing I did, because they found him. The paparazzi were hiding in the trees. They'd hiked in twenty miles to keep from being seen. His images went for a lot of money. I can't consciously leave you two there alone, but I promise to give you privacy."

The thought of privacy with Cash caused an ache in my belly. If Craig wasn't around, there was no telling what would happen. We'd flirted for so long, the sexual tension had been building for three years.

Back when we'd first met, he'd flirted with me, but I didn't take it to heart. I knew his kind, and I'd been in and out of enough venues with my brother to know how rockstars worked. Cash Roberts didn't fool me.

Now, things were different. We'd formed a friendship over the years, even though we continued to flirt. Since he'd come to Los Angeles, our harmless flirting had turned into kisses on the cheek, hands held protectively on my back, and a few stolen kisses when things were bordering on something sexual.

I'd had enough dreams of Cash Roberts between my legs over the years that I was primed for him anytime we were around each other. *Fuck, he was so damn hot*. So, whatever happened in Port Angeles was going to happen. I wasn't a whore, but if the opportunity presented itself, I was going to let Cash have his wicked way with me.

## Chapter 15
## Cash

The ride to Port Angeles was just under three hours by way of a ferry in Edmonds, Washington. Penny and I had gotten up early and were out the door by ten. We should be at my house by lunch.

Once Craig parked the SUV on the ferry, we were instructed to get out and go up to the passenger area and wait until we docked in Kingston. I'd made sure Penny had a hooded jacket and sunglasses for our trip. We'd need to be as covered up as possible. Someone would recognize her.

"Want something to drink?" I asked as we found a secluded area to sit. Craig put his big body in a chair that would block us both from being seen. I was comfortable with the ferry since I used it often to come to Seattle, and being seen wasn't as troublesome for me as it was for her. I usually got stopped by one or two fans requesting autographs. Penelope Keller was a household name already, and that didn't bode well for her.

"I'm fine," she promised. "We will only be here about half an hour."

Craig basically ignored us as we sat there, waiting for the short trip to be over. The Puget Sound was clear today and the sun was just starting to burn off the clouds. It wasn't supposed to rain, and I was glad. I wanted her to see how beautiful my home on the lake was when the sky was clear.

"I can't wait to go hiking," Penny whispered as other people started filling the area. No one looked over at us, and we made sure to keep our heads down, just in case.

"We can head out in the morning, if you'd like," I offered.

"Sounds good to me," she tilted her head just enough that I saw her smirk. "We are supposed to be decompressing, right?"

"Exactly." I returned her smirk and checked my emails.

There was one from the record label asking if we'd decided on the direction we wanted to go with the first release off the album. I stiffened in my seat. I'd been meaning to talk to Penny about starring in the video for the song we wrote about her, but it'd slipped my mind. I hadn't been able to think of anything else but keeping her safe since we returned to Seattle. I shot off a reply to them, saying I would have all the details for the videographer by Thursday, and leaned back in my seat.

"What's going on?" she asked, seeing my reaction.

"We can talk about it when we get back on the

road. It's business, and I don't want to discuss it here." I jutted my chin out at the other passengers who were milling about. The last thing I needed to do was say something within earshot of a person who would leak that to the press.

"Okay," she agreed. "Is it bad, though? You'd tell me if it was bad, right?"

"It's not bad," I promised, wanting to hold her hand, but I refrained.

Eventually, we made our way back to the SUV and climbed inside as the ferry was docking. Craig slowly rolled out with the other cars, then we were on the 104 toward Port Angeles.

"Okay," she said. "Are you going to tell me?"

"It's killing you not to know, huh?" I teased, hoping to keep the conversation light. What I was about to bring up might be a touchy subject for her.

"Well, yes," she groaned. "Now that you've made a big deal about it."

"The record label is scheduling our next video shoot," I admitted. "We will need to get it done before the album drops at the end of June. I know your schedule is going to be hectic, but I had an idea. I want you to star in the video."

"Wait, what?" she gasped. "Me?"

"Yes," I replied, taking her hand. I couldn't help myself when I reached up to cup her face. "They are wanting us to release "Purge" as our first song off the album."

"Oh," she breathed and stiffened. I rubbed my thumb over her cheekbone.

"You don't have to do it," I blurted. "You really don't, Penny. I just had a thought that it would be a good idea to shed some light on the disease. Maybe it would help someone suffering if they saw how far you'd come."

"Okay," she sighed. "What do you have in mind for the video?" I could tell she wasn't completely sold, and to be honest, neither was I. The last thing I wanted to do was bring up her struggle, possibly putting her back in that bad place.

"It would be simple," I began, dropping my hand from her face. "You would recreate your struggle and the scenes we plan would be cut and dropped between us playing the song."

"Do you want me to act out the purging?" she swallowed hard.

"I would never do that to you," I promised. "We can find a body double to act out those parts. At the end of the video, I would want you as you, showing how strong you've become."

"It could help someone," she said aloud.

"It could," I agreed. "But it could also bring up some things for you. Things I don't want to dig up if it would put you back in that place."

"No," she shook her head. "I won't ever go back to that person, Cash. The lingering medical complications are enough to remind me that I was young and dumb, trying to fit in to the mold of an industry I wanted to be a part of."

"We have a few days to discuss it," I reminded her. "Let's keep to our plan of relaxing until Wednesday. After that, we can give them the information to pass on to the producer."

"What about Braxton? Does he know about this plan?"

"He does," I told her. "He wanted me to talk to you about it. At first, he was against it, but once I told him my vision for the video, he came around. He said it was up to you, and that you would make the right decision."

"I'll think about it," she promised.

She relaxed in her seat as we drove. For the next hour, we didn't speak much, and eventually, she put in her earbuds and closed her eyes. I knew she'd need time to think about it, and if she did decide to go ahead, I would do everything in my power to keep her from falling down that rabbit hole again.

By the time we arrived in Port Angeles, I'd managed to reply to several emails and send the guys a group text, letting them know I'd talked to Penny.

They were happy she was considering it, and I told them we would make the final decision later in the week.

As we continued farther past the city, heading toward Lake Crescent where my home was located, Penny finally opened her eyes and stretched a little. She'd slept for about an hour and a half.

"We're almost there," I said.

She checked her phone as we drove, scrolling through email after email. I didn't pry, letting her take care of business. I kept my gaze out the window, watching the scenery go by. I loved the area, even though most days were not this sunny. There was a short break in the weather, and we'd have today and tomorrow without rain.

Living out here, it really didn't matter when you were used to the constant drizzle and overcast skies. It became part of life, and whenever I would be on the road, I actually missed it. Being out by the lake put me in a good place…much better than when I was living full-time in Seattle.

"The code is 1229. Just park in the front of the house," I told Craig as we arrived so he could punch in the code to my gate. The road made a turn to the left and to the right before the house came into view. It wasn't huge, but it was perfect for what I needed.

Craig followed the split in the driveway, taking

the circle drive to the front of the house. The other side would've taken him to my garage.

The dark brown, two-story house I'd bought was an investment. I'd spent a lot of time out here repairing walls and fixtures. It was therapeutic to do something with my hands right out of drug rehab. It kept my mind off of getting high.

"This is beautiful, Cash," Penny said in awe as she stepped from the vehicle. "Braxton said you bought it as a fixer upper."

"I did," I replied. "I'll show you around once we get settled."

We grabbed our bags, and Craig helped Penny with one of her suitcases. Hilda was there to open the door, welcoming me home.

Much like my condo, the foyer dumped you into a large living room with floor to ceiling windows, but this home was laid out quite differently. Hilda had a small room that was off the kitchen. She liked my home better because she had more room to move around than at the condo.

"I've made up the guest house for Mr. Huntley, and Ms. Keller's room is ready with new linens, as well." Hilda nodded and headed to the kitchen to our left.

"Let me get Penelope situated," I said to Craig. "Then I'll take you outside."

You could see my pool from the large windows, and the pool house was only steps from the back door. There were a ton of trees behind that, but one lone, winding path would take you to the lake where I had a boat dock I never used. I'd thought about buying a boat, but never did because we were always gone.

I placed my hand on Penny's back and took the suitcase from Craig, escorting her down the hallway to the right of the living room, bypassing the first staircase. "There are two ways to get upstairs, but these back ones are closer to my room and yours."

"Thank you for bringing me," she said, climbing the stairs.

I let her go first, and that was a bad idea. Her shapely ass was right there in front of me, her hips swaying with each step. I counted the sideways tilt as she moved. Fifteen steps later, she paused at the landing, turning around to catch me still staring at her. I didn't care, and obviously, she didn't either, because Penelope just laughed and pointed down the hallway. "Which room is mine, perv?"

"Perv?" I gasped, narrowing my eyes. "Baby, you haven't even begun to tap into my depravity."

"Mhmm, sure," she teased, turning on her heel.

"First one on the left," I offered. "Mine is on the right."

She opened the door, and turned around to lean against the frame. "I'll be down in a minute. Don't be peeking under my door later tonight."

"Penelope," I groaned. "If I wanted in your room, I would just barge in. No need to peek at you in your lace panties from under the door like some pubescent teenage boy."

She giggled and shut me out. I pivoted and adjusted my cock as I headed to my room. That woman was going to be the death of me.

## Chapter 16
## Penny

The flirting and sideways stares at each other had only gotten worse as the day wore on. By the time we'd finished dinner, I was a ball of sexual need. If Cash Roberts didn't touch me soon, I would be touching myself alone in my room, and I had no problem with being loud enough for him to barge through the door like he'd promised.

Craig and Hilda excused themselves and left us alone. I walked over to his white leather couch and grabbed the remote. Everything in the house was updated, modern. It reminded me of his condo, all minimalistic and plain. I never thought of him as a plain type of guy. There were no pictures or family mementos placed around the room, and it made me sad. He had nobody. No siblings or parents to claim. If it wasn't for the band, he would stay out in this wilderness without coming up for air.

"What has you so quiet?" he asked as he rounded the couch.

"Do you not have any photos of your mom?" I blurted, instantly regretting it. His eyes darkened, and I started to apologize, but he stopped me.

"I do," he sighed, pointing toward the staircase we hadn't used to go upstairs earlier. "There are several as you walk up."

"I'm sorry." God, I felt like the biggest idiot.

"No, it's okay," he said as he took his seat. "I don't talk about her much."

"Why not?" I continued. He was opening up to me a little more. I knew all of the basics about him, but the details were always left out of conversations.

"She told me to live my life to the fullest and to remember her, but not to mourn her." He paused to take a deep breath. "We were close, and she was all I had. After her death, I fell into the wrong crowd. I hid my feelings behind a bottle and loads of drugs. When I went through rehab, I also saw a therapist."

"You don't have to talk about it if you don't want to, Cash," I replied, and scooted over so I could touch him freely. He took my hand when I held mine out, and I squeezed it to give him some support. "I know how hard it is to bring up the past."

"She would've loved you," he whispered, and used his free hand to tuck a strand of hair behind my ear.

"I would've loved to meet her," I replied, letting my honesty show through my words.

Cash closed his eyes for a brief second and took a deep breath. He leaned in and pressed his lips to mine. I'd been waiting for the chance to kiss him again, and I wasn't disappointed.

My breath hitched, and when my mouth opened, his tongue swiped across my bottom lip, stopping to nip at the flesh. An ache built in my body, and I ran my hand over his knees, tightening my hold on his upper thigh when he cupped my face.

"Come to bed with me," he said once he released his hold on my lips. He wasn't asking, either.

I nodded and kissed him again, but he didn't make any moves to stand or grab my hand. My pussy was wet, and all of the sexual tension between us was making it worse.

"I want to hear your words, Penelope," he ordered. "I won't take you to my room until you say 'yes' out loud."

"Yes, damn it, Cash," I groaned. "Take me to your bed."

His body shot up, and as he pulled me to my feet, I saw the large bulge behind the fly of his jeans. *Fucking hell*. I was going to come just from my legs moving as we headed toward the back staircase.

When we reached the top, he spun me around, pinning me to the wall beside his bedroom door. My fingers tangled in his long, blond hair, and he pressed on my lower back so he could grind into the spot below my belly button but too far up from where I needed him to be.

I reached between us and cupped him through his

jeans. Cash let out a moan that almost brought me to my knees. He fumbled behind him and pushed the door open wide once he found the knob. We chuckled as he walked backward into his room while keeping his lips pressed to mine.

A light was on in the bathroom, and it shed just enough light for us to see where we were going. His bed was neatly made, but he changed that when he reached around me and tore the covers from their tucked in position. He lifted me and tossed me on the bed like a caveman, and I liked it…a lot.

He covered my clothed body and kissed me some more, falling to the side to take his weight off so he could cup my breast through my shirt and lace bra. I shivered when his thumb rolled across my hard nipple. "You like that, don't you?"

"Sensitive," I hissed as he did it again.

"Oh, baby," he smirked. "I'm going to have so much fun playing with you."

"Cash, you have got to touch me," I ordered. "I can't take this anymore. I'm about to explode."

"No, you're not," he teased and sat up, pulling his white, cotton shirt from his body. My tongue went instantly dry, and I placed my hand on his chest, feeling the muscles beneath. I'd always dreamed about what he looked like underneath those concert shirts and casual tees. Now, I knew, and I wanted to taste him.

My lips landed right above his heart, and he groaned from my attention. I cupped his cock again, and felt a bit of victory when he pushed into my hold.

"You keep touching me like that, and *I'm* going to explode. This will be over before it ever begins," he warned. He pushed my shirt over my head, and when I started to unhook my bra, he pulled my hand away and kissed the swells of my breasts.

"Cash," I hummed as he got closer to my nipple. I just wanted my bra off, and he could have his way with them. "Stop treating me like a princess. We both know I'm a brat."

Cash froze, his eyes raising from where he was focused on my nipple. His brows pushed forward. "I like you as a brat better, but don't push me, baby. Not right now. Not when I'm about to sink deep into that pussy. Be a brat later, because I have some punishments for you when you decide to talk back."

*Holy fuck!*

His mouth closed over my left nipple covered by lace, giving it a little nip to remind me that he was in charge. I liked it…I liked it a lot.

The sensation of the lace and his warm, wet tongue caused my fingers to dig into his thick shoulders. If I had to beg, I would. We'd had enough foreplay over the past few years through flirting, and I didn't need him to do anything other than fuck me.

I reached for his fly as he jerked my own. Our hands searched and touched and brought pleasure until we were naked, our bodies glistening with sweat. Cash's fingers slipped between my legs, rolling two of them over my aching clit, and he took my lips again with a fierce need when he felt how primed I was for him.

"Jesus, you're fucking amazing…beautiful," he declared as I reached for his cock. The man was…well, he was…yeah, he was thick…in all the best ways.

"Please, Cash, I need you inside me," I begged as my head tilted back as far as it could go.

"I'm not done tasting you," he mumbled around my other nipple. His thumb rolled across my clit, and I had to clamp down the urge to release so it wouldn't be over quickly.

He slowed his attentions as my body coiled and my moans became louder, eventually pulling his fingers from my body. I wanted to protest, but he pressed his lips to mine, sinking his tongue inside to tangle with my own as he pulled back, giving me a stern look. "Don't move."

He reached into the side table and grabbed a condom, his gaze never leaving mine. His eyes heated as he tore the package with his teeth and tossed it aside, rolling it over his hardness. I'd never been so turned on in my life.

He lurched forward and his fist landed right beside my head as he took his cock into his other hand. We didn't speak, because there were no words. I wanted to watch him; learn the signs of his pleasure.

His cock rubbed against my opening, and I felt the anticipation in my body. My hands landed on his sides, feeling the tight muscles beneath my fingertips.

As he leaned into me, we both cursed under our breath as he worked his way inside. It'd been two years since I'd been with a man. I hadn't had time for relationships, nor did I want one while I was making a name for myself in Hollywood. Being with Cash had been an unattainable desire because of my brother. Now, we were alone, and I'd given my body to him.

"I'm going to fuck you, Penny," he warned, drawing back just enough to make my body tighten around him. I didn't want him to stop. I needed the repetition of his strokes. "Kiss me, baby girl."

Although he ordered me as if I should take the lead, Cash laid his body over mine, moving his arms to where his elbows were next to my head. He interlaced his fingers on the top of my head and began to move as he took my lips.

My legs wrapped over his hips and I raised my

pelvis with each thrust. I was encased in him, his thick arms caging me in. I was helpless against him, and I wanted it. I wanted him to bring me to orgasm.

As he ground against me, my body primed itself for release. At no point did he touch my clit with his hands, because his body was doing it for him. I'd never come without help from touching my own body to achieve release. Cash was doing that without effort.

"Cash, I'm going to come," I finally choked out. "Oh, god..."

When my body released, his thrusts became punishing. My body accepted it, and it wanted more. As I came down from the release, he rolled and took me with him so I was on top. I adjusted my knees and took over, riding him ever so slowly.

"I can last all night," he smirked. He wasn't being cocky, and I somehow knew that. It was a warning, letting me know he was insatiable. I was going to make it my personal goal to prove him wrong. "Show me what you've got."

My hands reached for the headboard, and he cursed as my breasts hung right there in front of his face. I would use them to my advantage. He took one nipple into his mouth and I rotated my hips, eliciting another moan from him.

I felt his cock swelling inside me, and I knew he was close. Much like before, my eyes never left his. I let my body talk for me. As his own grunts got louder, I released the headboard and lay flat against his chest, taking his lips in a heated kiss.

His hips lifted as he grabbed my own. I held on to him as he thrust up into my body, finding his own release. I smirked into the darkness, not saying a word about driving him to the brink ahead of his own schedule.

"Damn it, Penny," he gasped at the height of his orgasm. "Your pussy is going to become my newest addiction."

## Chapter 17
## Cash

We left the house early. The hiking trail close to my house on the lake would take a couple of hours. Craig parked at the trail head and helped us out of the car. Penny had dressed in leggings and a tank top, but since it was still chilly outside, she wore a hoodie over it.

Once we reached the ranger's station, we all stopped to stretch. The hike was close to two miles round trip, but the views were breathtaking.

"Craig, I hope you are going to have a bit of fun today," Penny said as she leaned to the right to stretch her muscles. "I doubt anyone here will notice me or Cash."

"You never know," he shrugged. "Regardless, I've been wanting to get out and hike somewhere, anyway. So, yes, I will be enjoying myself today."

Craig gave her a rare smile and zipped up his raincoat. I'd already put my hair up into my beanie and was ready to go. We walked down a flat path, leading toward the trail. Once we entered, the trees made a canopy over our heads, stopping the drizzle from reaching us. The sword ferns and moss lined the trail as we descended into the forest. The wind didn't reach us here, and the cool, moist air felt weighted and eerie.

"Are you going to answer that?" I asked Penny as her phone began to ring.

"Nope," she said with her full lips making a popping sound. "I'm on vacation."

She reached into her pocket and retrieved her phone, shutting it off. Craig stayed behind us, and I held her hand. "We have today. If work calls for either of us this week, we have to answer it."

"Unfortunately," she sighed, looking up at the cover.

"Come on, let's get this hike done," I pushed.

The trail wound through the forest, ferns covering the ground on either side of the path. We got to the junction and Penny pointed toward the waterfall. We crossed a couple of creeks, and before we knew it, the trail had changed, creating a switchback up the side of a steep hill. The three of us jogged up the two-hundred-foot incline, and when we reached the top, I heard Penny gasp, "Oh, it's so beautiful."

The waterfall was at its fullest, and there was a little landing where we could stand and observe. She'd reached for my hand automatically, and I pulled her over to me as we stared at it in awe.

Craig gave us a few minutes alone, but we didn't need it. On the way back down to the trail, we saw a few people coming our way. Penny ducked her head as I did the same. Craig nodded when the group said hello, but no one said anything else as they passed.

When we arrived back at my house, Hilda was there with lunch, serving Penelope a salmon and spinach salad, and Craig and I had two fully loaded sandwiches.

"I need to power up my phone," Penny mentioned after Hilda came to take her plate away. "I have no idea who called me."

"Take your time," I announced as I stood. "I'm going to work on the information for the music video."

At the mention of the music video, we both paused. She still hadn't given me an answer, but I wasn't expecting her to until the last minute. What I was asking of her could bring up some horrible demons from her past.

"When do you need your answer?" she asked, jutting her chin out toward my computer. "Is that what you're going to talk to them about today?"

"I am talking to them today about the music video, but not about you. That's it," I promised, taking her hand so I could guide her to the couch. Craig and Hilda disappeared to their respective rooms. "I have to confirm the time and location where we will shoot. Your decision in this is solely up to you."

"What if I say no?" she pressed.

"We will have the body double do both parts," I replied. I wanted Penny to do the video, and yes, I was being fucking selfish about it. The song was written about her fight with bulimia, and it was only fitting she be the one to star in the video. Plus, it would really tell the media to fuck off once they saw what we had planned.

"Do you have a picture of her?" Penny continued with the questions, and I was going to answer each and every one of them to the best of my ability.

"I do." I nodded and released her hand, picking up my laptop where it sat on the coffee table. I pulled up the file I had on the video and found the headshots of the woman. There were several images attached showing her body in tight clothes and swimsuits from various photographers.

"She's pretty," Penny smirked. "With the right makeup, she would look almost like I did back then."

"I agree," I said, trying my hardest not to remember the images I saw online of a younger, sicker Penelope Keller.

"This woman is going to play me in the present tense, too?" she asked, her brows furrowing as she leaned in to stare at her.

"If it comes down to it, yes," I answered.

"She looks nothing like I do now," she noted.

It was true. The body double looked a lot like Penny when she was at her worst. Penelope had filled out and gained weight to make herself healthy. Instead of being a fucking skeleton, she had worked out and gained the muscle she needed to keep those curves I was addicted to. Her hourglass figure reminded me of those sexy pinup posters. A vision of Penelope with her hair up in those big curls, wearing a pair of tight, black, high-waisted shorts, a halter top, and pantyhose that bore a dark stripe up the back of her legs with heels danced through my mind, and my cock responded.

"No, she doesn't," I replied once I got my mind off of her in tight, sexy clothes.

"How will that work?" she continued. "If she is playing me before and after, it's not going to work, Cash."

"Camera angles, Penny," I replied. "I'm sure the producer will know what to do."

"Hm, okay," she mumbled, standing from the couch. "I'll be back shortly. I need a shower and a change of clothes."

I knew I had struck a chord with her. She left me alone to work on the information for the video, and I let her go. The one thing I'd quickly learned about her was she liked to make her own decisions. As much as

I wanted to protect and pamper her, she was a strong, independent woman. I had to trust her to make the right decisions.

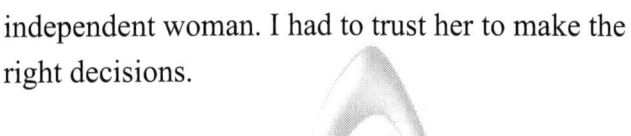

## Chapter 18
## Penny

I had to go back to Los Angeles on Monday. The call I'd missed was from my producer. She'd personally called me to let me know that a reshoot of the final sex scene with Malcom would need to be replaced. The first one didn't do the movie justice. I called her back.

"Harriet, it's Penelope," I announced when she answered.

"Look, I really, really hate to bring you back to work with that asshole," she said in a rush. "Especially since it's the sex scene. God knows I don't want to put you through that again."

"It's okay," I told her. "Can you email me the schedule?"

"Sending it now," she replied. I could hear her fingers dancing over the keys of her laptop as she worked to send me the dates. A second later, a ping sounded on my phone.

"I'll see you Monday," I said as a way of getting off the phone.

"Again, I'm so sorry," she repeated. "Now, I have to call that asshole and let him know."

"Good luck." I cringed when I thought of what Malcom would say when she called him.

Now, I had to get back into character and plan a fake romantic fling with Mr. Asswipe. The thought made me sick. It was hard enough the first time, and now that I'd had sex with Cash, I wouldn't be able to keep a straight face when I faked it with Malcom. Cash had ruined me for any other man I ever filmed with or dated.

The thought brought me up short. What was going on with us, anyway? We weren't dating. Hell, I didn't even know if what we'd done the night before was simply because we'd given in to the years' worth of flirting.

If we did try to make a go of whatever this was, how would we even make it work? He had to tour, and I'd just signed the remaining contract for the rest of the series to be made into movies over the next two and a half years. That was a lot of time to be apart from one another.

With the news I'd be going back to work early, I didn't know how that was going to affect the filming for the band's video. I really wanted to do it, and I should probably call my agent. If I knew Paul, he'd urge me to do it for the exposure. As much as I liked Paul, he was always okay with a little drama mixed in to keep my name in the press, but at least he wanted the headlines to read good news. I would've fired him if he'd been okay with all of the negativity and hate

I'd gotten over the last few years.

Firstly, I needed to talk to Cash and let him know about my schedule after I took a look at the email Harriet had sent me. Secondly, I needed to know more about the video. If the idea he'd presented was done in a sensitive light toward bulimia like he said, then I was willing to do it. Seeing the body double play me at my worst was going to be hard, but my brother and Cash would be there for support. I didn't know how they did it when they were on tour and saw other people using drugs.

It was hard to overcome addictions, as well as mental disorders. God knew I'd been through enough depression to last a lifetime. Therapy helped a lot. I realized I finally had something to live for; a goal to reach. It wasn't just my movie career goal, either. I wanted a loving partner and maybe, just maybe, further down the road, a child.

The only thing holding me back from bringing another human being into this world was the fact that I didn't want him or her to go down the same path my brother and I took in our younger years. It was too stressful to think about it.

As I sat on my bed, I felt a pressure in my head. A pain bloomed behind my eye. I took a few calming breaths, but I knew it wasn't going to stop the migraine that was coming.

"Fuck, not now," I groaned. I needed water, and I needed to close the curtains so I could crawl into bed.

My hand reached for the door, pulling it open a little too hard. I hurried down the hallway to get to the kitchen. I covered my left eye with the back of my hand as I entered the living room, and I heard Cash call out my name as I passed. Just the sound of his voice made the pain behind my eye worse.

"What's going on?" he bellowed as I grabbed a bottled water out of the fridge.

"Shhh." Dear god, his voice was so loud. "I need to take some meds and go to my room. Can I close the blinds in there?"

"Migraine?" he asked quietly.

I nodded and started walking back the direction I had come, but his arms around my waist slowed my steps.

"My room can be darkened better," he whispered. "Come on, let me get you into the bed."

"Hurry," I mumbled.

We reached his room, and I immediately crawled into the spot closest to me, pulling all of the pillows around my body. With the anxiety of knowing the headache was coming, I just wanted to be bundled up. I blindly reached for a pillow as I heard the blinds being closed.

"Meds," I mumbled.

"Where are they?" he whispered as he touched my cheek.

"Bathroom counter," I replied.

I heard his footsteps leaving the bedside, and I closed my eyes. The pain was becoming unbearable. I knew the medicine would help, but I needed to sleep the rest of the pain away. It hurt too much to talk, and I hoped he would understand if I didn't move for a few hours.

"Sit up for me, baby," he cooed as he entered the room. As I sat up, Craig was standing in the doorway, keeping his back to most of the light coming from the hallway. I still squinted as Cash dropped the pill in my hand and handed me the bottle of water.

"Sleep," he ordered. "I'll come check on you in an hour."

I could do nothing more than nod as he let me cover my head with a pillow. I hated the headaches, but it was a part of my life.

Cash closed the door, and I felt myself drifting off after the medicine started to work.

I felt the bed dip as I came awake. The pain in my head was gone, but I was careful not to open my eyes. Cash's hand slipped over my hip, and I felt his warmth as he spooned up behind me.

"Cash," I moaned as I removed a pillow from over my face. His lips touched the back of my shoulder, and I smiled when I felt his hand brush against my arm.

"You've been asleep for almost three hours," he informed me. "Are you any better?"

"Yeah," I swallowed. My throat was parched. "I think so."

"Hilda made dinner if you're hungry," he whispered. "I can bring it in here."

"No," I sighed, finally opening my eyes. The room was still pitch dark, and I wondered how he had made it to his bed without sight. "I need to get up."

"What can I do?" he asked. I heard the worry in his voice, and I rolled over to face him. I buried my face into his neck and inhaled his scent. Whatever it was, it made me want to wallow in it so I could smell like him.

"I need a little light, please," I admitted. "I need to gradually get my eyes to adjust, or I'll be right back in the bed."

"Okay," he said, kissing my forehead. "I'll crack the bathroom door and get some light in here."

"Thank you."

When the light came on, I spent about ten minutes letting my eyes adjust. Thankfully, I didn't have any sensitivity, and I was especially thankful I didn't want to vomit. In fact, my stomach growled, and I placed my hand over it to dull the sound.

"I need food," I chuckled.

"Let's head to the kitchen," he suggested. "Hilda has everything ready."

"Cash, wait," I blurted, stopping him from letting me go.

"What is it?" His brows pushed forward, and I didn't miss his gaze as he quickly inspected me like he would be able to diagnose what was wrong with me.

"My producer personally called me earlier," I began. "I have to be back in Los Angeles on Monday to reshoot a scene."

I cringed internally when I remembered what we were going to have to do.

"How long will you be there?" he asked, and I heard the caution in his voice. He wouldn't be able to go with me. Cash had his own work to do, then there was the music video.

"Just a day or two, hopefully," I sighed. "I have to reshoot the sex scene with Malcom."

I expected him to say something, maybe even yell, but he didn't. Instead, Cash sighed and pulled me tighter to his body. I didn't miss how his muscles molded perfectly to my curves.

"Are you okay with that?" he finally asked.

"I have to be, Cash," I answered. "It's my job."

"I know it is," he replied. "I also know how you

feel about Malcom."

"He's a douchebag, and he will bitch the entire time, but he knows how important this movie is," I stated. "If he wants to get it done as badly as I do, then he will play his part and we could be done by Monday night."

"I can't go with you," he complained. "I'd rather be there so I could keep an eye on him, but I have to get prepared for the music video."

"About that," I began. "I've been thinking. I'd like to do it, because I don't think the body double would do my present body justice."

"I'm glad you want to help us," he said, kissing my lips just once, but that one peck was full of fire. "I want you to be comfortable with everything, though."

"I think I'll be fine," I promised. "If I can make it through several sex scenes with Malcom, then I can do just about anything."

Cash's eyes narrowed. "Several? How many times are you fake fucking Malcom in the movie?"

"We shot four scenes," I admitted. "I don't know if they'll all make the cut, though."

"Jesus," he chuckled. "I'm competing with a fictional character."

"Competing?" I asked, confused.

"I've only had you once," he smirked. "I guess we are going to miss dinner, because I need to get a leg up on ole Malcom."

I laughed as he pushed me over on my back, but the sound was cut off as he kissed me, making me forget about my fake boyfriend waiting for me in Los Angeles.

## Chapter 19
## Cash

It'd been four days since she had left with Craig at her side. I'd paced the floor of my condo in Seattle for the past hour, waiting for her to arrive. The moment the door opened, I was standing there with my arms opened wide.

"I'm so glad that's over," she gushed as she melted into my embrace. I didn't even respond to her. My lips did the talking as we stood there making out with no cares in the world. I was so lost in her, I didn't even care Craig was trying to get around us to drop her bags off in her room.

"I missed you," I admitted, pulling her by the hand.

"I missed you, too," she replied, removing her hat and glasses.

"Why were you so late getting here?" I asked once we made our way into the living room.

"Ahh," she replied, shaking her head. "Well, they found us at the airport, and Craig tried to lose them when we were heading this way. Thankfully, they didn't get into the parking garage."

"Shit, they followed you?" I growled. The damn paparazzi were vultures, and I hated them with a passion.

"Yeah, but we are okay," she promised.

"Good," I sighed as Craig returned. Hilda was working in the kitchen, preparing dinner for everyone. I had her hold off until they arrived so we could discuss the music video shoot over dinner.

"So, tomorrow, huh?" Penny asked as we all took a seat.

"Yes," I said with a nod. "We have to be at the location at ten."

"Honestly, I'm very excited about this," she told me. We'd talked about it more while she was in Los Angeles. She'd come around a lot easier with the information I had given her.

"I am, too," I replied.

We ate dinner, and Hilda and Craig left us alone for the evening. Penny was at the kitchen table working on her social media posts while I shot off a text to the guys about some last-minute things before the shoot. We'd be filming our portion of the video where we would be performing the song in a warehouse to fill in the storyline. We wanted the focus mixed between the two.

"Fuck," Penny gasped.

"What?" I asked as I came to her side. "What's going on?"

"This." She cursed again and pointed to the screen. An email had come in from her admirer, Ed.

He'd expressed his love of how she looked as she left her hotel in L.A. each morning, and he wanted to know if she would finally meet him for lunch in Seattle while she was home. "Is he following me?"

"Let me get Craig," I growled, feeling panic in my chest. "Stay here."

I looped off toward the bedrooms and knocked on his door. He didn't waste time answering, either, because I knew my knock could've woken the dead.

"Show me," he ordered without even asking me what was going on.

We returned to the kitchen, and Craig leaned over Penny to read the message. He asked her to forward it, and then he placed a call to a guy named Roger. He told the guy what was said in the latest email, and asked Roger if he'd found anything. There were some nods and pacing, but eventually, he hung up the phone and took a seat.

"Roger is my I.T. guy," he began. "He's found Ed, but the guy has no background. He lives in Los Angeles, and he's been making a few trips to Seattle, but that's all we know. There are no hotel records, either."

"What does that even mean?" Penny asked. She looked at the email again and shivered.

"He could be smitten with you," Craig said. "This happens a lot. Most of the time, they will give up and move on once the newness of their obsession wears off. Other times, they will do anything in their power to get close to you. At that point, they may just want a picture and five minutes of your time, or they will get dangerous. Right now, you are protected. The security at the condo is top notch. They won't let anyone get in the building who doesn't belong."

"I don't want to meet this guy, even if it's for five seconds," she worried, and I totally agreed with her.

"Roger is sending me his photo," he announced as he checked his phone. "I want you to study his face. If you see him anywhere we go, I need to know immediately."

"Of course." she answered. I wanted to memorize this asswipe's image, too.

Craig set his phone down on the table in front of Penny. As she studied the image, I leaned over her to get a good look at her stalker. He was in his forties, maybe closer to fifty. His dark brown eyes looked haunted, though. It could've been his jet black hair, but I thought I'd seen him before.

"I've seen him," I barked as realization hit me. "Holy shit, Penny. That's the guy who was working security at the studio in Los Angeles."

"That's not Mr. Thomas," she reminded me.

"No." I shook my head. "This guy was there the

second time I came to visit you. He was working the door. I swear it was him."

"I never saw him," she frowned. "Are you sure?"

"One hundred percent," I growled, knowing this motherfucker had been so close to her before she had security.

"Good news is that it's over," Penny said as she slumped in her chair. "I don't have to go back."

If this guy was making frequent trips to Seattle, he knew more about her than he had let on in his emails. Thank fuck Craig had been there with her over the last few days.

"Everything is going to be fine," Craig promised as he pocketed his phone. "The video shoot is tomorrow, then we need to plan Penelope's press tour. I'm bringing in two more men for those appearances."

"Good," I agreed. "We have a little over two months until we head out. Maybe this guy will settle down before then."

"I sure hope so," Penny replied.

## Chapter 20
## Penny

Cash and I arrived at the warehouse to shoot the music video, and my brother was already there. He pulled me to him in his usual brotherly hug, but this time, he held on a little longer. "Are you going to be able to do this?"

"Yes," I nodded as I stepped back. "I know exactly what needs to be done, and I'm okay with it, Brax. It's time I do something to make a difference. I have a voice now, and I can't hide from the media forever. I think your song and my presence in the video will send a strong message."

"As long as you are okay with it," he pressed.

"I am. So, stop worrying." I poked him in the side and turned toward Cash, who was walking over with the woman who was going to play my body double.

"Penelope, this is Marlow," he introduced.

"Nice to meet you," I said, sticking out my hand. She gave me a genuine smile and shook my hand.

"We really do look alike," she stated, and I felt my brother tense beside me. I ignored him, because she was right. What she said wasn't hurtful.

"The producer would like to meet with you both to go over what he has planned," Ace announced as he approached. "After that, I guess you two will go into makeup while we film our part of the video."

Everyone separated as they headed off toward the area where the band's crew had already set up their mock stage. A guy I'd never seen before was working on the lighting while the producer pointed out things to his cameraman.

Cash wrapped his arm around my shoulders and turned me to face him. "I'm going to be right off camera the entire time."

"I really wish everyone would quit worrying about me," I said through gritted teeth. "I'm fine, and I'm going to be fine."

"Okay," he replied as his head dipped, pressing his lips to mine for a soft kiss. "I trust you to come to me if you are having a hard time."

"I promise you, I will." I returned his kiss and cupped his cheek, stroking his freshly shaved face twice before letting him go. "I've dealt with harder things than this, Cash."

"Penny, you inspire me to be the best person I can be," Cash admitted. "I see you surviving, and it gives me hope I can, too."

"You can survive, as long as you don't let your demons rule you," I reminded him. "We have to live this life, and we only get one shot at it."

"Not only are you beautiful, but you're smart,

too," he chuckled and kissed me one last time.

When we broke away, he took my hand and guided me over toward his producer. My brother was sitting behind his drum kit, and his eyes were following us. He'd kept his opinion to himself about Cash and I spending time together, and I gave him a soft smile, hoping he caught my gratitude.

What Cash and I had was more than the flirting we'd done over the years. He and I just clicked. He understood my past, and I knew his, too. Being with him was just…easy. Like breathing. I was falling for him, and it was coming on fast.

"Eric, this is Penelope Keller," Cash said as we approached.

"Very nice to meet you, Ms. Keller," he said, shaking my hand. "Marlow is waiting in that office by the door, if you are ready. I'll sit down with you both and give you some instruction as to what I'm envisioning. After that, I will start with the band, and we will shoot your parts in about two hours."

We followed him to the office, and we sat at a round table. Cash leaned against the door frame and listened in. I glanced at him occasionally as Eric rambled on about his ideas. I really didn't need any guidance since we were basically retelling my own story.

I knew Cash had written the song, and the lyrics

would punch you right in the gut if you paid attention to them. It wasn't just Eric's vision, it was Cash's, too.

Marlow and I were taken into another office that was set up for makeup. The guys exited a third office after changing into their clothes for the shoot, heading for the set. Cash had already changed, and I tried to keep my eyes off his tight black jeans, white cotton shirt, and leather jacket, but it was hard. Seeing him dressed for the stage always caused a flutter in my lower belly.

As I sat in the chair, I heard the song come on over the sound system they were using. The guys would perform the entire song, and our parts would be added in. I didn't know exactly what was going to be used, but I knew it would be amazing.

I was done with hair and makeup before Marlow. They were making her look sick, using some old photos of me to copy what I'd been going through. When they started darkening the spots under her eyes, I stepped out. As good as I thought I was at seeing it, the first glance gave me a bit of anxiety. She really looked just like I had at my worst.

I closed the door softly and walked back into the main warehouse where they were resetting the area to do another take. Cash's eyes landed on mine as he adjusted his bass strap. There were questions in his eyes, but a short shake of my head gave him enough peace to know I was okay.

Was I okay?

Maybe, yes. Fuck, I really couldn't tell if I was or not.

A flash of black hair turned my head, and I saw Coraline enter from a side door. She hurried over toward me and pulled me into a hug. "It's so good to see you, Penny."

"How are you? How's the baby?"

"She's wonderful," Cora beamed with pride. "Taylor is a great dad, but I had no doubts."

"What are you going to do this tour?" I asked. Coraline was their tour manager, and I had no idea what she was going to do now that they had a child.

"I'm sitting this one out," she frowned. "We eventually will hire a nanny and take April with us on the road, but right now, she's just too young. I need to be here with her."

"That's good," I replied. "I'll be gone until the movie comes out. After that, I should be free if you want to get together."

"I'd love that," she grinned. "We will need a girl's night while the guys are gone."

"Will Presley be home anytime soon?" I asked.

"She will be off tour while the guys are on," she sighed. "I think she might go with Ace for a while, but she promised me she'd be home for once."

"I'd love to just be normal for once," I pouted, and Coraline placed her hand on top of mine. I gave my head a little shake. She understood and backed off. At least she wasn't voicing her concern over the nature of the video shoot.

After the band was done, Eric took me out back, and in the alleyway, he'd set up lighting. The idea was for me to walk toward the camera as if I was walking a red carpet. At the end of my walk, when I hit the mark he'd placed on the ground, I would look into the camera and give it a little smirk like I was telling everyone that I'd won.

On the other side of the building, he'd set it up to look like I was stepping right into a hoard of paparazzi. That was to be filmed twice. He'd enlisted about ten of his friends to pretend to be the press. Marlow would walk out as the old me, covering her face in shame, and I would walk out as I am now, but with my head held high. The two clips would be put together to show the difference in the two times in my life.

When he called for quiet, I glanced over his shoulder, and sure enough, Cash was there like he'd promised. My gaze leveled on the producer and his cameraman. When he gave me a nod, I took a deep breath and got myself into the headspace I needed to act. Only, this time, I wasn't acting out a part for a fictional character. I was playing myself, and this was the part where I took pride in my accomplishments.

"Action!" Eric called out.

I walked toward the camera and at the end, I gave my smirk. We filmed that scene three more times to get several different angles and reactions. When we were done, I hurried into the dressing room and changed into an outfit that matched Marlow's.

My heart sank in my chest as she moved during her part. I didn't know how she did it, but she mimicked me to a T. Every step looked like my own, and I was in awe of her skills by the time she was done.

"How in the world did you do that?" I asked.

"I studied you on YouTube," she replied, but placed a hand on my wrist. "I am amazed by you, and I look up to you. Not many people could've done what you did and still land a major leading role in a movie. I know Hollywood can be tough, but you are tougher."

"That's so sweet of you," I said, trying my best to keep from tearing up. I still had to act out my part.

"I can't wait to see how the video turns out," she cheered. "You nailed that walk in the alley."

She was there? I was so focused on Cash and doing my part, I hadn't even noticed I'd had an audience.

"It's going to be great." Our conversation was cut short when Eric called for everyone to get back into place.

When I walked by the paparazzi for the next part of my shoot, I tried to ignore them, but in the back of my mind, I knew that was my new reality. Especially after the first movie dropped in just a couple of months. I wouldn't be able to hide away in Cash's lake house anymore.

By the time we were done, it was after ten at night, and I was exhausted. Eric finally sent us on our way, and Craig was there in the alley with the SUV ready to go the moment Cash and I walked out the door.

We made it to the condo and I went straight to Cash's bed, barely remembering to change into something comfortable to sleep in. The music video was done, and so was the film. I just wanted to rest for the time being, and deal with my new life later.

## Chapter 21
## Cash

*Six weeks later...*

"We have four days before you fly to Miami," I groaned as her pussy clamped down on my cock. I'd tasted every inch of her as I held her hands above her head. "I need more before I have to leave."

We'd spent the last several weeks hidden in my lake house, and if it wasn't for the need for food, I'd have kept her in bed the entire time.

"Yes, more," she moaned as I leaned into the restraint I had on her hands.

"You like this, don't you, baby?" I cooed. Fuck, when I'd held her like that for the first time a few weeks ago, her pussy had gotten wetter and she came almost instantly.

"I would like more than this," she replied with heat in her eyes. "I'm not fragile, Cash."

"Your sass should get you gagged," I teased, but it wasn't a tease. I would take one of my few silk ties and do it if she'd let me. I liked her submission, and from the way she was rolling her hips, I knew she liked my dominance.

I was by no means a sadist nor was I a Master, but I liked to play a little rough in the bedroom.

"You're playing with fire, Mr. Roberts," she teased back.

"I like your fire, baby," I said, leaning down to take her lips. My thumb rotated her clit just enough to get her body to coil, then I let it go. Her heated curse was like music to my ears. "Do you want to come?"

"Only if you will allow it…Sir," she flirted.

"A gag and a spanking later," I promised as I resumed rubbing circles around her little nub. I could still taste her on my tongue, and I was getting addicted to it.

"Promise?" she asked, closing her eyes as I added a little pressure to my attentions. Her hands tightened around mine as she undulated underneath me.

"Come for me, baby," I panted, feeling my own release building.

Her shout of ecstasy spurred me on, plowing into her as she begged me to go harder. I'd already learned her body, and there was a special place inside her that begged for attention when she came. Her eyes closed, her nails dug into my arms, and her breasts heaved with each breath she sucked in between her teeth as she begged for more.

My release hit like a fucking freight train. There was no drug in the world that could replace what my body experienced every time I was with her. She was my new addiction, and I couldn't get enough.

My lips crashed down on hers as she moaned again. I rocked in and out of her until my softening cock slipped from her body. I yanked the condom off and tied the end, dropping it to the floor.

She cursed when I buried my face between her legs. I wanted every last drop of her release. With my tongue, I coaxed another smaller release from her, and I relished in the feeling of her thighs clamping around my head. If I died between her legs, I'd die a happy man.

"Mr. Roberts?" Hilda called out as she knocked on the door. Penny gasped and reached for the covers to keep our housekeeper from seeing her naked, but I knew Hilda wouldn't enter without permission.

"Yes," I called out.

"Ms. Keller's brother is here," she informed us, making Penny push me away so she could scramble to her feet. The look of terror on her face made me chuckle.

"Tell him we will be right there," I said through the door.

"Oh my god," she whispered. "Fuck. Damn it! He's here."

"It's okay, Penny," I laughed. "Your brother is smart. He knows we've been doing it for a while now."

"That's not funny, Cash!" She whispered a scream, and I caught myself laughing again. She threw my pants at my face and ran into the bathroom.

I left her to clean up and used my fingers to comb out my hair before leaving the room. I knew I was joking with her, but I still didn't want to rub it in Braxton's face that I was fucking his sister.

"Hey, Brax," I greeted as I came into the living room. He was standing with his back to me while he looked out the windows.

"Where's Penny?" he grunted.

"I think she's cleaning up," I replied as he followed me into the kitchen. "Are you hungry?"

"No." He waved off my offer. "I wanted to see her before she left."

I nodded and poured myself a glass of orange juice. He kept glancing down the hallway, and I knew he was wondering what was taking her so long.

"Braxton," I sighed, pointing to the table. "I'd like to talk to you before she gets in here."

He grunted again and took a seat. We faced each other, and I was thankful for the space between us, but that didn't mean he wouldn't come across the table when he heard what I had to say.

"Look," I began, rolling the half-empty cup between my palms. "Penny and I…well, we've become closer."

"I already know," he admitted. "Look, I didn't want you being with her. She's my sister, for fuck's sake. But you treat her like a goddamn queen. I've never seen her this happy."

"Jesus, I thought you were going to deck me." I was relieved to say the least.

"Oh, I will if you fuck her over," he replied, his eyes narrowing on me. "She's not like the other women you've been with."

"I agree." I nodded, but held up my hand. I wanted him to hear me out. "Penelope is everything I never knew I needed. I have feelings for her, Brax. Solid, hardcore feelings."

He quieted and stared at me for several seconds. I had no idea what he was thinking, but I hoped it had nothing to do with his giant fists and my pretty face.

"Do you love her, Cash?" he finally asked. His eyes were still narrowed like he could see into my mind to make sure what I was admitting was the truth.

"I think I do, Braxton," I admitted. The "L" word had been rolling around in my brain over the past week or two, but I didn't know how to approach her with it. Was it too soon? Maybe, hell…damn it…I didn't know.

"If you do, you better not fuck it up," he warned, pointing in my direction. "No fucking around on tour.

No flirting with the women at our shows. No lying, cheating, and you sure as fuck better not fall back into your addictions. She can't handle her own, let alone yours, should you start using again."

"I have no fucking reason to do drugs again, Braxton," I gritted out through my clenched teeth. "I know I have a history. She knows everything, and I mean *everything* about who I was. Just like I know everything about her."

"Treat her right," he whispered as he stood when she came out of the hallway.

"Penny," he called out as she came over to hug him.

"What are you doing here?" she asked, casting her eyes toward me. I was sure she was looking for any indication her brother had blackened my eye or something.

"I came to see you before you left," he told her.

"I'm not leaving until Thursday," she scowled. "What's going on, Braxton?"

"Nothing," he hedged. Who was lying now?

"Oh, don't start that shit with me," she scoffed, placing her fist on her hip. My cock threatened to harden at her sass. Fuck! I loved it when she did that. "We're twins, remember? I know you better than anyone."

"I honestly came by to see you," he vowed,

placing a hand over his heart.

"Mmhmm," she replied, coming over to take a seat next to him at the table.

"Do you have everything ready for your trip to Miami?" he asked, changing the subject. She narrowed her eyes for just a second. When she realized he wasn't going to tell her anything else, she sighed and nodded.

"Craig is having two more security guards in place there for when we land," she announced, rubbing her forehead. I watched her carefully to see if she was heading for a migraine and was relieved when she dropped her hand. "Knowing my life is changing so fast is kind of scary."

"It's going to be scary," I blurted. "You've taken the precautions you need to keep yourself safe, though. Craig isn't going to let anyone hurt you." And if he did, I would kill him.

"I agree with Cash," Braxton said, reaching over to take her hand. "You have to start thinking like an A-list celebrity, Penny. You have to plan everything you do from now on, and with the contract for two more movies in this series, it's only going to get more hectic."

"The only thing I'm grateful for is the fact that at the end of book two, Malcom's character is killed off. I don't think I can handle two more movies with him."

All three of us burst into laughter, and it calmed the mood in the air. Hilda came in and asked if Braxton was staying for dinner. When he declined, she disappeared into her quarters.

We spent another hour talking and preparing Penny for her solo trip for her press tour. We had our own tour starting in two weeks, and I needed to get my things together, as well. I left them to talk as I went into the living room where my three bass guitars sat in their cases. I'd had one of my crew, Liam, bring them from storage. I needed to change out the strings and polish them up the way I liked them before we left.

I ignored them as they spoke softly behind me. The last thing I wanted to do was bother them while they were having family time. Every so often, I would hear them talk about their mother, and I smiled. I always liked Mrs. Keller, and she had been so nice to Ace, Taylor, and myself when we'd brought Braxton in as our new drummer. It felt weird having a mother figure around, but she made it easier because she basically adopted us from that first day.

I glanced up at the picture above the gas fireplace in my living room. Penny had urged me to move it from the unused stairway. My mother, with her long blonde hair, stood there next to a tree in our old yard.

I didn't know who had taken the picture, but I knew it wasn't my father.

I'd never considered myself a mama's boy, but I did give her credit for a lot of the good things about myself. All of the bad things I did, I associated with my father. It'd been a hard go at life, but I made it. I just wished she was still here, because she would've loved Penny.

## Chapter 22
## Penny

The moment the wheels touched down in Miami, I squared my shoulders and walked off the plane with my backpack and bodyguard at my side. Craig rushed me out to a waiting SUV, pushing the vultures with their cameras aside so I had a clear path to the vehicle. A man opened the door and shielded me as I climbed in the back. Inside was a man dressed in an expensive suit, much like the man holding the back door, with a white button-down shirt and dark sunglasses.

"Penelope, this is Ellis and Quinn," Craig said in a rush, as the first guy jumped into the front seat. Their names sounded like last names, but we didn't have time to get into the specifics. "They're going to take you to the hotel while I get our bags. I'll be right behind you."

On my nod, he closed the door and we were off. I didn't know which one was which, but when the guy in the passenger seat turned, I recognized him from the picture Craig had shown me on the plane. He'd prepared me for just about anything.

"Ms. Keller, my name is Brian Ellis," he greeted and lifted his glasses so they sat on top of his head. "This is Mason Quinn. We have checked into your hotel, and the manager is letting us use the service elevator whenever you need to come and go for the interviews."

"Thank you, both," I said. "Please, call me Penny. I need some normalcy in my life right now, and calling me Ms. Keller makes me uncomfortable."

"Okay."

I leaned back in my seat and watched as we took the interstate toward the hotel. I'd never been to Miami, and I wanted to take in all I could in the short amount of time I was going to be there. If Cash was here, I would've loved to spend some time on the beach with him, but he was back in Seattle getting ready to fly to New York for their first concert.

The music video was being released tonight, and so far, no one had let it be known that I was starring in it. If anyone followed the band and knew I was related to Braxton, they could probably put two and two together and realize the song that was released last week was about my eating disorder.

We pulled up to the back of the hotel, and Ellis hurried out to open my door. I scooped up my backpack and walked beside him to the service elevator. We took it to the fifteenth floor and stepped off. He produced a key and waved it over the panel in front of the door to our right and pushed it open wide to reveal a suite that appeared to be twice the size of my old apartment.

I made my way into one of the three bedrooms and dropped my backpack on the king-sized bed. The window looked out over the ocean, and I felt a little pang in my heart when I realized I couldn't share it with Cash.

I was seriously falling for him, but our lives were going to be tough if we wanted to make it work. With him touring and me being in all kinds of places to film, would we be able to see each other enough to keep up a strong relationship?

There were ways. Hell, Ace and Presley were doing just fine, and they were constantly touring in different cities. She'd called me the other day, and we'd talked about it after I had asked her how she and Ace were handling the separation. She promised me it was okay to be worried, but to keep a steady line of communication open with him, and slip away whenever I had two days off.

"Hello," I sang as my phone vibrated in my hand. My heart leapt in my chest when the picture I'd assigned to his number came up on my screen.

"Hey, baby," Cash said. God, his voice sounded like honey. "Did you make it okay?"

"I did," I promised. "There were a lot of cameramen at the airport, but the hotel was empty because we came in the back door."

"Good," he sighed with relief. "I miss you."

"I miss you, too," I replied.

"We will be in New York late Wednesday," he reminded me. "I'll have Hayden bring me to your hotel Thursday as soon as Craig gets him the information."

"I know I land around noon," I advised.

"That's enough time to spend with you before the show," he confirmed. "You have your interview on Friday morning. After that, we are going to have to find some time to see each other before we meet up in Dallas."

"I have my schedule," I reminded him. "I don't know if it's better for me to come to you, or for you to come to me."

"It's easier for me to come to you," he admitted. "Your face is all over the news right now, and I don't want to risk you being out in public with Ed still lurking around."

"I haven't heard from him in weeks, Cash."

"Still, it doesn't matter," he scolded. "Your safety comes first."

We talked for the longest time, and I finally hung up the phone when Craig knocked on my bedroom door to let me know food had arrived. "I'll call you before the video drops," he said as a goodbye.

When I entered the living room, the three men

had changed into more casual clothes. I'd been too busy talking to Cash to get out of my black pantsuit. "What's on the agenda for tomorrow?"

I took my seat and opened the lid on the plate Craig had ordered for me. I gave him a thankful nod and took the first bite of salmon as he removed his phone so he could go over the sheet from the movie review site that had requested interviewing me first. Malcom was going to be at this interview, and I dreaded being in his presence again, but it was the nature of the beast. Only three more weeks until the premier, and after that, we had eight months before filming the next movie where he would die a slow, painful death. I couldn't tell you how excited I was that movie three would be with someone else playing the male lead.

"We have to leave the hotel at twelve-thirty to make it to the studio at one," he began. "Hair and makeup will take about an hour, and the actual interview is scheduled for two. We won't fly out of Miami until Sunday." Today was Friday.

That gave me a week to finish up the interviews with movie bloggers and reviewers until I had to be on national news Friday around eight in the morning. Cash's show would be the night before, and I knew I was going to be exhausted, but I was willing to do that so I could see him perform.

The New York show was already sold out, and I couldn't wait to see them live again. The new album was breaking records already, and it had just dropped. They'd worked hard to reach the level of popularity they were experiencing, and I couldn't be happier for them.

"I'll set my alarm for nine," I advised. "I'll need a little coffee to wake up."

"The hotel has a small gym if you'd like to get a workout in tomorrow morning, too," he informed me.

"I'd like that."

After dinner, I took a bath and stayed in there until right before Cash called. We'd scheduled the music video to drop at five that night, Seattle time. It was nearing eight on the east coast, and I grabbed my laptop once I was dressed in a pair of shorts and a tank top. My phone rang exactly five minutes before the top of the hour.

"Are you excited?" I asked him as a greeting.

"I am," he replied, but the other end of the phone went silent. "How are you?"

"I'm relieved it's finally coming out," I said. "I hope it shows the media that I don't care what they say about me."

"Good, baby," he sighed. "It's almost time."

"Let's do this," I chuckled.

## Chapter 23
## Cash

I buckled my seatbelt on the plane as we took our seats. Ace and Hayden were sitting next to me while I stared out the window. Braxton and Taylor were with our second security guard, Marshall. The crew had departed a few days ago to get ahead of us to set up for the first show in New York City. We'd tour across the United States and Canada for the next three months before heading to Europe to finish out the tour.

My knee bounced as we waited to takeoff. The flight attendants were doing their last-minute checks and getting those of us in first class a drink while we waited for everyone else to board. Like always, we declined alcohol and waited until it was time to fly.

The only thing keeping me from going insane was knowing we'd land late in New York, and by the time I woke the next morning, I'd be that much closer to seeing Penny.

She'd been doing her press tour for the movie during the afternoons, and we talked for hours in the evenings. If I didn't love her before she left my bed in Washington, I knew for sure I loved her now.

After takeoff, I closed my eyes and slept for most of the flight. When we landed, we were met by a few photographers, most of them asking about Penny and her involvement with the music video. Hayden and Marshall rushed us to a waiting SUV and we were off to the venue where our tour bus was waiting for us.

The video had been a hit, and our song was picked up by national satellite radio the first day. The tabloids had, of course, speculated and upped their search for her, taking pictures of her at every stop on her press tour. I watched the websites almost obsessively, and it was a good thing she did not. They'd brought up her bulimia, reposting pictures of her from four years ago. I didn't want her to regress back to those times, and a few text messages to Craig assured me she was doing just fine.

Food was waiting for us when we arrived at the venue, and we all ate before unpacking our belongings on the bus. When I finally found a quiet enough space to call Penny, she was half asleep when she answered.

"Cash," she yawned.

"I'm sorry, I didn't know you were asleep," I cringed. "Call me tomorrow."

"Okay, night," she mumbled. I hung up the phone and headed back to the bus just as thunder rumbled overhead.

I had twelve hours before she arrived, and it took everything I had not to stare at the clock. I needed

Penny in my arms, and I wanted her underneath me. It'd already been too long since I had been inside her.

We'd hired on a new crew, leaving Liam to take over the tour manager position Coraline had held before she had the baby. They'd been setting up our new stage since earlier in the day. We'd headlined shows before, but this was going to be our first arena tour. The excitement was overwhelming at times.

As the bus settled down, I worked on social media posts, thanking the fans for the one million views of our new video. There'd been so much positivity toward Penny and what we'd created that it restored a little bit of my faith in humanity. The media was another story. They kept dredging up her battle, but we'd seen so many women, and men, come forward with their stories. Maybe, just maybe, we could really make a difference in someone's life.

By three in the morning, I was tired enough to climb in my bunk, waking up when Liam gave me a little shake.

"Huh?" I mumbled.

"It's nine thirty," he announced. "We have to leave in thirty for an interview."

"Okay," I mumbled and dropped from my bunk. I jumped in the shower and brushed out my hair, giving it a quick dry before bundling it up into a beanie.

Ace, Braxton, and Taylor were drinking coffee in the front living area of the bus when I met them, and I glanced out the window. The rain from the night before had stopped, and I breathed a sigh of relief. Penny would be landing in a few hours, and I didn't want anything delaying her arrival.

"Penny called me this morning," Braxton announced.

My cup stopped halfway to my lips. "Is everything okay?"

"She's on her flight now, but she said the press was at the airport," he cursed, wiping a hand over his face. "I'm happy for her, but I'm also worried."

"I'm worried, too," I replied as we both gave each other a knowing look. "Hayden is taking me over to meet her at the hotel at noon."

"Ellis and Quinn are already on the ground with a vehicle for her and Craig the moment they land," Braxton advised us. "She has her interview tomorrow on the morning news."

"What time is sound check tonight?" I mumbled over my coffee.

"Four," Ace piped in.

"I'll be here," I grunted and stood. "Let me grab my things and I'll be ready to go."

The next two hours were full of interviews, an acoustic performance for the radio station, and a thirty-minute autograph session when we left the studio because we were met with a hundred or so fans. By the time we got into the SUV, I leaned my head back and sighed.

"Well, boys, we're on the map again," Ace cheered.

The four of us pounded fists. We'd been so close to this status all those years ago, but we blew it because of our addictions. Being clean was good for us, and as I looked around at my bandmates, I could tell they were thinking the same thing.

I tried to not check the time on my phone every ten minutes, but I failed. Penny was arriving in a half an hour, and Hayden was going to drop everyone at the venue before taking me over to her hotel. When we arrived at the bus, I placed my hand on Braxton's wrist to stall him from leaving. I needed to have a heart to heart with him about my feelings for Penny.

"Hayden, could you give Braxton and I a moment?" I called out as he parked. Our security guard nodded and slipped out of the driver's seat. When I turned to look at her brother in the seat behind me, I could tell he already knew what I'd planned to say, but he didn't stop me from talking. That had to be a good sign, right?

"Look, I want to talk to you about Penny," I began. "Things have gotten serious between us."

"I know," he grunted. "I've talked to my sister."

"I know you didn't want me around her because of my past." I swallowed. "I've changed, Braxton, and Penny has grounded me even more."

"Do you love her, Cash?" he asked with narrowed eyes. "Do you *really* love my sister? Because the last time I asked you, you hesitated."

"I do," I agreed immediately. "I love her with everything I have, Braxton. We've grown in our friendship, and that means something to me over all the other stuff. Your sister gets me, and she trusts me with her past just as I trust her with mine."

"I wanted to keep you two away from each other, because of your past," he sighed. "Penny has a strong will to do as she wants, and I can't blame her. I'm the same way. But…she's different with you. Not a bad different. It's the opposite. I see her smile more. She holds her head higher, and her confidence is top notch, my man. If you are the reason for that, I'm not going to warn you away from her. She needs someone like you in her life."

"I will protect her for as long as she will keep me around," I vowed, reaching over the seat to offer him my hand. When he took it in his strong grasp, we shook and I felt the tension release. She was mine and her brother approved.

"Now, go see her, and bring my sister here before

the show starts," he ordered with a rare smile. "I've missed that little shit."

My laugh echoed in the SUV as he made his way out to grab Hayden. I melted into the seat as we headed for the hotel. It was only a matter of minutes before she was going to be in my arms.

I couldn't wait.

## Chapter 24
## Penny

The moment I walked in the door to my hotel room, I saw him standing there. He wore his usual tight, ripped, black jeans, an old concert shirt that'd been torn to hell, and black boots. He was dressed the part of a rockstar about to tear up the stage, but instead, he was there for me.

"Cash!" I squealed and dropped my bag by the door. We met halfway and the moment he cupped my face and took my lips, I almost cried. Not because of our reunion, but because I wanted to tell him everything that'd happened that morning. The details of it would have to wait because the moment Hayden closed the door, we were ripping at each other's clothes.

"God, I've missed you," he breathed against my lips.

"I've missed you," I replied and looped my arms around his neck, pulling him back to my lips. I wasn't done kissing him yet.

"Come to bed with me," he ordered, taking my hand. My shirt and shoes were on the living room floor of the suite right next to his boots and shirt. I'd barely gotten the button undone on his jeans before he couldn't take it much more. The large bulge in his jeans let me know he missed me, too.

He entered me swift and sure. My body didn't need to adapt to him, because it remembered his attentions as if we'd been together the night before. God, I really had missed him.

The stroke of his cock was slow, and while I wanted to make it last, my body had other ideas. I lifted my hips to let him dive deeper inside me, hitting the spot that triggered my need for release.

When he released my lips, Cash curled his back so he could take my nipple into his mouth, biting down on it with just enough pressure to send me over the edge. I didn't need to speak, because my moans and movements told him everything he needed to know.

As my body relaxed, he smirked and pulled out, using his hand to urge me over onto my stomach so he could take me from behind. His cock was still hard as steel as he entered me again. I didn't think I could rebound from my first release, but he proved me wrong.

"If this is how we meet each other after being apart for some time, I will meet you anywhere," he groaned as he fell to the side, pulling me toward his body so we could spoon together.

"I've been thinking about this all day," I admitted and wiggled my backside against his cock. If he wanted to go again, I was willing.

"You have to get ready for the show," he reminded me.

"When do we need to leave here?" I asked, rolling to face him. I traced the lines of his face with my eyes, but that wasn't enough. I had to touch him. It'd felt like years instead of days since we'd last seen each other.

"I have sound check at four," he explained. "So, we should be out of here by three. That'll give you time to see your brother." His lips held a smile when he brought up Braxton. I already knew Braxton was aware we were seeing each other, but did he know how serious we were?

"I see he hasn't killed you yet," I observed.

"We talked," he replied, his smile even wider.

"I'm guessing by your smile, things went well?" I dared to ask.

"Actually," he said, cupping my face and placing one kiss before backing away. "I told him that I was head over heels in love with you, and that I would protect you as long as you kept me around."

"Wait, what?" I grinned. "You love me?" My voice took on a teasing tone, but inside, butterflies were dancing in my stomach.

"I do, Penelope," he sobered. "I really do, and if you'll have me, I want you to be mine…permanently."

"I do," I nodded. "Cash, you complete me. I don't know how you do it, but you are there for me through everything. Even my past doesn't faze you. How could I not love you?"

We kissed again, and those kisses turned into more lovemaking. By the time we cleaned up, Hayden was knocking on the door to the suite, letting us know it was time to head out. We held hands all the way to the venue.

My brother was the first to greet me, but my eyes kept flickering to Craig. He'd always kept to his stiff stance when he was around me, but today was different. I had learned to watch him for little differences that told me when things were okay…and like now, things were not as he liked. I still hadn't told Cash or Braxton what had happened before we left the airport, and from the look on my bodyguard's face, I knew I needed to come clean.

"Can we go inside and talk?" I asked.

"Sure, what's going on?" my brother replied with narrowed eyes.

Craig made a move to open the door of the bus, jutting his chin out for Cash to follow us onboard. My brother and lover exchanged glances, and by the time I took a seat on the small dinette, they were pacing.

"What happened, Penelope?" Cash growled. He

only used my name when he was serious.

"So, when we arrived at the airport, Ed was there," I announced, but held up my hand. "Everything is fine, but we had a scare."

"What did he do?" Braxton bellowed. "If that motherfucker touched you."

"He didn't," Craig interrupted. "But it was close."

"Close, how?" Cash asked.

A shiver rolled down my spine at remembering what had happened. We'd arrived to a volley of press waiting for me to exit the blacked-out SUV. The moment I'd gotten away from them and into the airport, a commotion to my left startled me.

"Quinn and Ellis were on her flanks as we entered the airport," Craig began. "I was in the lead, protecting her from the front. We'd just cleared the glass doors when someone reached out to grab her. I heard her gasp and turned around to reposition her when I saw Quinn knock a man's hand away from her side. Ellis and I pulled her close, but she called out my name when she recognized who it was. From the tone of her voice, I knew exactly what was happening."

"Was it that fucking Ed guy?" Braxton vibrated with anger, and when I glanced at Cash, he wasn't doing much better.

"Yes, we made a positive ID on him, and the local authorities took him away." The door opened and Ellis and Quinn stepped onto the bus. Both of them looked like they had some news to share, too.

I really wanted to forget about my little stalker. Ed was dangerous, but at least he didn't pull a gun on me or my bodyguards.

"We have news," Quinn announced.

"Tell me," I ordered. "Did they arrest him?"

"Oh, yeah," Ellis smirked as he nodded. "Ed had warrants. He's been known to stalk other female celebrities, but he'd been caught on camera breaking into a singer's home last week and stealing about fifty-thousand dollars' worth of jewelry. He's being held on grand theft charges, and I don't think he's going to be able to post bond."

"Holy shit," I gasped. "That's going to put him behind bars for a while."

"Yes, it is," he nodded. "He's been stalking more celebrities than just you. So, he won't get off easy."

"Thank god," Cash sighed and came over to my side, taking my hand to pull me from the seat. He pressed his lips to mine and cupped my face, like he always did, then he pulled away. "I'm so glad you listened to me and hired them."

"Me, too, Cash," I replied.

"Sound check time, boys!" Liam announced as

he climbed the stairs.

We all followed the band into the arena, and I watched from the side of the stage as they worked through a song to get everything ready for the night ahead. It was their first show to kick off their newest album. I couldn't wait for the real show to go on later that night.

When the curtain finally fell at ten p.m., I sang along to the songs they performed as I watched the crowd go crazy. Cash was only steps away from me, but he kept focused on the crowd until it was time for them to play my song. He glanced over a few times, and every single time he did, I kept a bright smile on my face to let him know I was doing okay.

My time with bulimia was over. I loved myself the way I was, and I'd found a man who loved me just the same. I didn't know what our future held, but I knew I wanted to be with him for the rest of my life.

Epilogue
Cash

Penny and I married in Vegas before she started filming the second installment of the trilogy. We'd taken the band and her mother to the city for a long four-day weekend over the fourth of July. Granted, we didn't do anything traditional. In fact, we married on a whim.

"So, I guess everyone wasn't surprised we would fly them to Vegas so they could watch us basically elope," she chuckled as the limo pulled away from the little wedding chapel just off the Las Vegas Strip.

"Your brother asked me why I didn't marry you sooner," I said with a roll of my eyes. Her brother had become our biggest supporter. As much as I wanted to say I didn't care what he thought, deep down, I really did. Braxton and I had grown closer over the course of our tour, and when we arrived back in Seattle, we had been inseparable. Abby and Penny were best friends, and there wasn't a thing the four of us didn't do together.

"He doesn't have room to talk," she chuckled. "He and Abby waited almost a year."

"True," I replied. "Enough about them. I want us to not leave the bed for the next two days. I don't want to miss a moment with you before you have to leave."

"Agreed, Mr. Roberts," she hummed.

"I love you, Mrs. Roberts," I teased. She would keep her stage name as Penelope Keller, but legally, she'd take my last name. I didn't care either way as long as she woke up next to me every morning for the rest of our lives.

We hurried over to our suite at the Mandalay Bay and spent the next two days making sure we got lost in each other before she had to head out on location to Costa Rica to film the opening scenes for the movie.

"I'll fly down in a few days," I reminded her as we reached the airport in Vegas. She would get to the location, and after I handled some things for our next tour, I would split my time between her filming locations and our tour.

"I can't wait," she promised as I kissed her goodbye.

Her lips were red and swollen by the time Hayden, Quinn, and Ellis escorted her through the doors of the Las Vegas airport. Hayden pulled away from the curb and took me back to the hotel where I'd meet my band and get things rolling.

The news has spread of our nuptials, and for once, the media showed us in a better light. Nothing was said about her bulimia or my drug use. The world was happy for us, and although it didn't matter, I was thankful we didn't start our forever off on anything negative.

# About the Author

## About Theresa Hissong:

Theresa Hissong is the bestselling author of the Rise of the Pride series. She writes paranormal romance, rockstar romance, and romantic suspense.

She enjoys spending her days and nights creating the perfect love affair, and she takes those ideas to paper. When she's not writing, Theresa spends her free time traveling and attending concerts all over the United States. Look for other exciting reads…coming very soon!

# Other Books by Theresa Hissong:

Fatal Cross Live!
Fatal Desires
Fatal Temptations
Fatal Seduction

Rise of the Pride:
Talon
Winter
Savage
The Birth of an Alpha
Ranger
Kye
The Healer
Dane
Booth
Noah
Taze

Morgan Clan Bears
Mating Season
Mating Instinct
Mating Fever

Incubus Tamed
Thirst

Standalone Novella
Something Wicked

Book for Charity
Fully Loaded

Club Phoenix
The Huntress

Cycle of Sin on Tour

Rocked (A Rockstar Reverse Harem Novel)

Printed in Great Britain
by Amazon